ALIVE

ALIVE:

Their Beginnings

Emily Prisk

Charleston, SC
www.PalmettoPublishing.com

Alive: Their Beginnings

Copyright © 2019 by Emily Prisk

First Edition

Printed in the United States

ISBN-13: 978-1-64990-075-3
ISBN-10: 1-64990-075-9
ISBN: 978-1-64990-074-6 (eBook)

To Western Christian High School in Upland, California, a community where the Word of God is honored and spoken of as the highest authority. A body of believers who are equipped to share the love of God with the world. A school where its students are given the highest caliber of education. An ever-growing heavenly family that welcomes everyone as worthy masterpieces, created in the image of God. Western Christian High School is this and so much more. Without this school changing my life, this book would not exist. Happy one hundredth year to my beloved school!

TABLE OF CONTENTS

CHAPTER 1

ZOOM IN

Darkness shall never overcome the light. This dark night in particular, one pale gleam of moonlight had just snuck past two separating gray clouds in order to light the path of a gloomy, abandoned street. As the ray came ever nearer, one lonely traveler could be seen in its light, wandering this rarely traveled sidewalk. Surrounded by abandoned slums, piled trash, and broken concrete, the traveler walked with his head held low. Known by very few as Kyle, he fit the definition of "needy" to the letter. His shoes were covered in holes, and his thin legs were half bare as his oversized brown shorts, which he could barely keep on his body, ended before his knee. Above this his tattered, oversized gray jacket had too many holes to keep him warm on this cold October night. These were the only clothes he had to his name. With his hood covering his face and headphones, which he wore in order to pretend he had a phone inside his pocket while on the most dangerous side of town, Kyle lifted his head and stopped suddenly in the shadow of a crumbling brick warehouse.

All the old buildings around him were a bit better than a pile of rubble, but this warehouse seemed to be the most intact. It rose above the other buildings to the size of some great mystical dragon in the dark of that night. Its windows were broken, its exterior was falling apart, and its entirety was swallowed in darkness. With a look of fear, he took off his hood and revealed his scrawny young pale face and shaggy long black hair. He remained staring at the worn, cold brick building for a moment. After gulping very hard, he slowly went closer. Very determined and very quick-paced, he made his way to the back of the building. In the black of night, a dim light shone from the entrance of the warehouse's underground basement. The frightened boy gulped again and, trembling, found the first crumbling step down into the basement. Each step he descended brought him further into the basement, and as he descended he could hear voices and laughter growing ever louder and louder and more and more defined.

Once finally inside, he was not at all surprised to see the basement was filled from wall to wall with loud men, women, and children. It was so crowded that people stood shoulder to shoulder all around. Their varied conversations and spouts of angry shouting and scary laughter became incoherent, bloodcurdling chatter. The men and women cursed and drank, while the teens and children, both girls and boys, yelled vulgar things about one another and started fist fights with each other. Besides being filled with people, the room was coated with an unbearable smell. It was the scent of stale beer, mold, sweat, cigarette smoke, and other unappealing smells too horrible to mention. Those who were smoking cigarettes and cigars filled the air with their smoke to the point that the room became engulfed in a thick haze. The floor was basic concrete, but the trash, goo, spills, and mess that covered it made a carpet of stickiness and wetness so thick that no one was able to see the concrete underneath it all. As if the people in attendance weren't loud enough, in the farthest corner of the room stood a giant speaker booming out songs made up of cursing and violence. The room was very dimly lit with a few scarce light bulbs that hung from the ceiling. In the center of the room stood a small makeshift platform made from broken boxes and tables taped together. The people in attendance inside this basement were known to the area as their local gang.

Kyle had just snuck his way into the doorway of the basement and was sitting atop a beer keg when a twenty-year-old man hopped up onto the center platform. His head was shaved and covered in tattoos, and he wore low hanging jeans with no shirt. His one gold tooth shone when he smiled, which he only did when he was planning something big and illegal for his gang to do. He was the gang's leader, and this night he was grinning from ear to ear because it was initiation night.

"Tonight our boys become men!" he chanted, and the room exploded with cheers. "Come and earn ya place!" he called as he took a moment to spit on the dirtied concrete. With the command, young boys from all over the room came up onto the homemade stage, all except one. Suddenly, people throughout the crowd began to give each other strange looks as if something was wrong. Somehow the crowd knew one was missing, and after looks were exchanged all around, Kyle was spotted and pushed up to the front. With a nervous and trembling grin, he stood up there with the rest of the boys with his hands in his pockets.

"Tonight we show them Bible thumpers where we stand!" the leader motioned for applause once again, and the boys knew what they had to do. The next hour, six boys were marching down a street in the night, holding spray paint and laughing, all of them except one. Kyle seemed the only one who was nervous, and he was the only one without a spray paint can. He was given a special assignment because he was the oldest of the boys at thirteen. While the other boys tagged the church that tried to minister to the people of that area, it was the eldest's job to steal one item from the church and bring it back to the leader of the gang. When they finally came to the church, they all became completely silent. What met the boys in the night was three long, narrow buildings. The first building stood all the way to the left and was a two-story office building lined with windows on the top floor and doors on the bottom floor. It was called "building one" by the congregation and had the parking lot to its left. On its right was a narrow concrete alleyway. On the other side of the alleyway, facing building one, stood another two-story office building that was identical to building one. This building was called "building two," and to the side of building two, with its right side facing the public and its door facing the parking lot, stood the main church building. This building was where the congregation met every Sunday. It resembled a small white house lined with stain glass windows, with a steeple and a cross on top.

The boys darted left and right, finding walls to cover in graffiti. Meanwhile Kyle had noticed something the others didn't. The church was completely dark except for one small light that shone from an open door of building two. This gave Kyle an idea, and he decided he would mug whoever was in that room and take their wallet. He crept slowly in the great big shadow of building two, putting on his hood and making sure to stay with his back against the side of the building in order to not be seen. He felt this job would be fairly easy for him, and he thought that it may get him props with the gang leader when he told him how he got the wallet. Either way, Kyle looked less confident when he noticed the person inside turn off the light, come out, and lock the door. The person coming out was a tall and well-built man, and the wannabe thief knew if he was going to take his wallet, he would have to take it now by surprise instead. So as soon as the man turned around, Kyle bolted forward. In the darkness, he misjudged how far away the man was and ran right into him. In a second, both the man and the boy fell to the ground, the man dropping all of his belongings as he fell. This was the wannabe thief's last chance. Panicking, he scrambled in the dark to find something of worth of the man's to take. Suddenly, his hand touched something small, rectangle shaped, and leather. The image of a wallet popped into Kyle's head, and he grabbed it and bolted away from the church. "Run!" shouted one of the other boys, and they all followed Kyle back to the warehouse basement.

"Idiot!" shouted the gang leader as his goons threw Kyle into the street. When he had finally made it back to the basement, he was met by cheers and celebrating from the men and women around. "Show us what you got, boy!" called the leader with a big grin. Proudly, Kyle strode up to the makeshift stage and reached into his jacket pocket. With his head held high, he boldly took out the rectangle and handed the leader what he had stolen. In the light of the basement, he now saw with horror what he had grabbed: a small leather Bible. The leader's expression turned from gladness to anger in a matter of minutes. Without a word, the leader pulled out his switchblade and slashed Kyle's left ear. Kyle fell back onto the floor, holding his now-bleeding ear. That's when the leader's goons grabbed him. "Worthless! Get outta here! And take your book with you!" the leader yelled as Kyle fell into the dirty street. With a laugh one of the leader's goons threw the Bible at Kyle's head and closed the basement doors behind him. Then, as if on cue, it started to rain. Angered and saddened, Kyle jumped up to escape the rain, leaving the Bible on the ground. He took five running steps and turned to look at the book that had lost him his chance at being in a real gang. The book looked small but important as it now sat on the concrete being covered in rain. With a roll of his eyes, he gave into his curiosity, though he didn't even know why he cared about a book. He grabbed the Bible, stuck it in his jacket pocket, and ran back into the night.

Kyle had no real home to go to. The place he had been calling home for a year now was a mattress and a stool that he guarded inside an abandoned, broken-down apartment building. His little space didn't even have a door and was merely three walls and a crumpled heap of brick outside in the elements. He ran into his shelter to escape the rain and threw the Bible onto the stool with a thud. "Dumb book! It's your fault!" he yelled as he plopped down on his mattress. His ear throbbed and continued to bleed profusely. He threw his hands up in the air and let them land with a thud back on the mattress. Suddenly, the storm clouds outside merged together and hid the stars from view. Since Kyle's shelter hadn't had electricity in years, everything around him was plunged into night's blackest shadow. His hand fell to his side, where he kept a small flashlight, but he didn't turn it on. He sat in the dark feeling awful. Kyle was a boy on his own. He wasn't known by many people, and he didn't know a lot about the world around him. He usually just did what felt right, which usually meant that he, lots of times, did whatever he wanted to do. Doing whatever he wanted to do when he wanted to do it left Kyle's life to be blown about by chance. He never could be sure what tomorrow would be like. Also, being so alone always left Kyle feeling vulnerable, isolated, and frightened at times of having something happen to him and no one being there for him. Being in the gang would have given him more than just bragging rights and protection out on the streets. It would have given Kyle, or so he thought, what he truly craved: to be known. Now seeing how quickly the gang leader disposed of him, he felt truly forgotten, truly alone, truly without direction, truly lost.

With nothing else to do, he picked up his flashlight, turned it on, and aimed it at the Bible on the stool. He stared at the Bible for quite some time, until he finally broke the silence with a groan. "Why'd it have to be a book! Couldn't I grab somethin' cool, like a watch or a purse! Why'd it have to be a church! There ain't nothin' at a church!" he yelled out loud in an angry tone. "What am I supposed to do now!" he huffed. He sat in silence for a moment, hearing the rain hit the concrete to his left and wondering when it was going to be sunny again. He wasn't tired; in fact he was wide awake from all the excitement and fear he had just gone through, not to mention his being drenched from head to toe. After staring at the book a little while longer, he rolled his eyes once again, gave into his boredom, stood, and grabbed the book off of his stool.

He jumped back down on the mattress and made it shake. Then he reached for his flashlight and opened the first couple pages of the Bible to the book of Genesis. "I got nothin' else to do." He groaned as he read the title out loud. "Genesis? Weird name?" As he finished the first couple of paragraphs, he sat back and spoke out loud. "The Earth was in darkness? Empty? That's how I feel," he thought as he read. "God, who is that? It says He created everything? That means He created me too. Since God created me, then He knows me!" Kyle reflected, and he continued to read the entire book of Genesis, and the entire book of Exodus. It took him a few hours, and he had many questions. "Where do I fit in all this? Why did they eat the fruit? What is the fruit? What happened to Moses?" were just a few of the many questions running through his head. Once he finished the book of Exodus, a bookmark fell out from in between the pages. It was a beautiful bookmark with a picture of a sunset on it and the verse John 3:16 written in cursive. At this point Kyle had found out how to work the Bible's table of contents and out of curiosity turned to the Gospel of John. The rest of the night, he spent reading book after book, Gospel after Gospel, until morning. That morning, when the sun rose in the sky so did Kyle's heart as he realized many new realities. "There is a God" was the first reality to hit him that night. "God made us, and God's Son is Jesus" was the second, and "Jesus loves me, He died for my sins, and He wants me to follow Him" was the third. He hadn't figured out everything there was to know about the gospel, and he was very confused still on a lot of things, but he knew one thing for sure. "Jesus would want me to return this," he said to himself, and with that, he got up and made his way back to the church he had visited the night before.

The morning he decided to return to the church just so happened to be a Sunday morning. Kyle found a place behind some bushes where he could see the church without being spotted. He saw that no cops were around nor any yellow police tape as he had expected. Instead the church was operating as normal with its churchgoers lined up at the door to receive their bulletins. He figured the man he had stolen the Bible from would be inside and that he could return it to him sneakily somehow once inside.

He ran over, pulled his hood over his head, got in line, and tried to go unnoticed. "Hello!" beamed a young girl handing him a bulletin at the door. She had bright red curly hair, purple glasses, and a flowing white dress on, that sparkled in the sunlight. She was the same age as Kyle, though she held herself more poised than he did. "Pastor Stanson has prepared a wonderful sermon today!" she said happily. Since he was the last in line, she didn't mind starting a conversation with him.

However, Kyle didn't want to talk. He kept his head down, quickly grabbed a bulletin, and muttered "thanks." With that, he ran inside and looked around. He expected that whoever lost their Bible would be raving about it somewhere and that's how he would recognize him, but he didn't get the chance to listen to the people's conversations. For as soon as he entered the church, the older lady who played the organ beckoned everyone to rise and begin to sing.

Kyle rapidly found a seat in the back row and nervously tried to look like he knew the words. After three songs, everyone sat down, and the pastor made his way to the pulpit. He was a tall older man with full gray hair and was dressed rather neatly. "Good morning, everyone! I know you have all noticed the new artwork that now covers our walls, but it's nothing a little paint can't fix! I was starting to think that the buildings needed a new coat anyway!" began the pastor, and all the congregation laughed. "That was not the only thing that happened last night. In the night, I was robbed. Someone ran into me and stole something very precious to me."

Kyle held his breath. "I stole from the pastor! Outta everybody, it just had to be the pastor!" he thought as he sank in his chair in anguish.

"That something was my Bible, and I just hope that whoever has it, the Lord is having it move in their life as it has in mine." The pastor then continued to explain how the graffiti was a result of them sending people over to the dangerous part of town to minister there and how the church should be glad they were chosen to be singled out in this way because it meant that the church's ministry was making a noticeable difference in the community. Kyle wasn't listening to this. He sat the rest of the time in dread and dismay at what he and the boys did that night. By the end of the service, Kyle was sure he was not brave enough to go up to the pastor and confess. So he decided he would have the cheerful red-haired girl simply give the pastor back the Bible for him. He met her outside and asked, "Yo, could you give the pastor this back from me?"

He went to hand her the Bible, and after staring at it in his hands for a moment, she smiled and said, "Oh no! You have to give it back to him yourself! He will be so pleased to meet you!" Without any notice, she grabbed his hand and pulled him back into the church right as the last parishioner was leaving. "Pastor Stanson!" the girl called as she pushed Kyle up the aisle toward the pastor on stage. When the pastor saw the young boy, he knew right away who he was from the ashamed expression on his face. With a look of his eyes, he signaled for the girl to leave them, but before she left, he mouthed, "Thank you very much," to her.

"So you're the book thief!" the pastor said with a grin. Kyle's heart fell, and he gulped hard.

"Yeah, I'm sorry," he said in a squeak. He really wanted the pastor to like him. "I brought it back," he said hopefully and handed the small Bible to him.

"Keep it." Pastor Stanson shrugged. "I have twenty Bibles, some of them in other languages. Say! What's your name, son? Don't worry, I'm not going to call the fuzz. This can just be between you and the Lord and me." With that the pastor sat down in one of the pews and motioned for the boy to sit next to him.

Kyle obeyed and said more calmly, "My name's Kyle. I heard you sayin' somethin' up there about a dude named Paul? You said he used to be called Saul? Why did he get a different name?"

"Well, his name changed because he was changed. Tell me, were you listening to my sermon?" the pastor asked kindly. Kyle nodded his head yes. "What did Saul do in Damascus?"

"He became not blind; that was awesome. He was baptized, and he told people about Jesus."

"Does that sound like a guy who wants to kill Christians?"

"No," Kyle answered as he tried to understand what the pastor was telling him. He sat for a moment and stared at his feet, thinking hard. Then he looked up at the pastor and asked, "How did he change? I mean, what's this all about?"

"Well, it all started when God created the world."

"Hold up, what started?"

"Everything. God created everything, and He made the first ever man, named Adam."

"I read 'bout Adam! God made him; then God made a girl. Then they ate a fruit that they weren't supposed to, and they had to leave," Kyle said, attempting to remember what he had read the night before.

"Yes, so Adam and Eve sinned."

"Huh?" Kyle interrupted, confused. The pastor paused for a moment.

"Let me try this another way. Who has never done one wrong thing in their life?" the pastor asked with a smile.

"Huh?"

"Who is perfect?"

Kyle stared forward, wondering if this was a trick question. He turned and looked the pastor in the eye and said in an uncertain tone, "Nobody? Everyone does bad stuff?"

"Exactly! Now, God has set up a law."

"The commandments?" Kyle interrupted the pastor. He knew about the commandments from his reading in Exodus.

"Yes, good job! The commandments and the rest of the law. Now, when people rebel against God and go against His law, this is called sin."

"But last night I read some of the commandments, and there's no way anybody could not do all that stuff!" Kyle yelled, interrupting the pastor once again.

"You're right. On our own, we, everybody on the whole planet, is doomed because we are all sinners. The punishment God has set up for sin is death and separation from Him. For God is a Just God and a Holy God. But here, open to the Sermon on the Mount," the pastor said, quickly grabbing the small Bible from the boy's hands and speedily turning through the pages.

"Why?"

"Because my bookmark is there because I can never remember where the beatitudes are located. There! Now read this," the pastor said, removing the bookmark from its place and handing it to Kyle. It was a handmade paper bookmark, colored with crayon and created obviously by some small child in the pastor's life.

Kyle read the title on the bookmark. "Romans, number five, dots, number eight."

"That's Romans chapter five, verse eight," the pastor corrected.

"Oh?" David continued reading the bookmark. "But God demonstrates his own love for us in this: While we were still sinners, Christ died for us." David paused and thought a minute; then in a frustrated voice, he huffed, "I don't get it!"

"Well, in order for us to be reconciled to God, God sent His son, Jesus Christ, born of a virgin, to be a sin offering for us," the pastor said matter-of-factly.

"Wait, an offering?" David asked, interrupting the pastor for the third time.

"In order for there to be forgiveness, there had to be the shedding of blood, but that's next week's sermon. For the time being, you must understand this. That Jesus Christ, the Messiah, became fully human and fully God. He died on a Roman cross after living the one and only sinless life," the pastor explained.

"He didn't do one sin!"

"Nope. He was sinless. He was perfect. So since He was without sin, He did not need to die, right?"

"Right?" answered Kyle. "So why did He die?"

"He took our place. He took our punishment for the sins of the entire world. He took the sin of the whole world on Himself because He loves us and wants to make us His own."

"That's a lot of love."

"You're telling me, son!"

"Then what happened?"

"Then Jesus rose from the grave, showing He had triumphed over death. Then He ascended into heaven, and one day, He will return to judge the world. Now, those who believe in His name and His resurrection can be forgiven by God and reconciled to Him through Jesus Christ and His death on the cross. We can have a relationship with the God that created heaven and earth, and those who believe in His name and His resurrection can have eternal life with Him." Kyle paused and gave a sad expression. He thought about all the sins and bad stuff he had done in his life, and hearing that those things separated him from God made his heart grow sad and heavy. Pastor Stanson noticed the boy's expression, and he put his arm around him. "Listen, Kyle, do you want to be forgiven by the Lord?" Kyle looked up at him hopefully and nodded his head yes.

"But what do I have to do? How do I know I'm forgiven?"

Pastor Stanson turned in the open Bible to Romans 10:9: "If you declare with your mouth, 'Jesus is Lord,' and believe in your heart that God raised him from the dead, you will be saved." Kyle's face and heart lifted. "If you sincerely believe that Jesus is the Son of God and that He died for your sins and was raised from the dead and if you ask Him to forgive you and to be the Lord of your life, He will, and you will have eternal life with Him. He is the one who saves us. He knows your heart. Kyle, would you like to pray for your salvation?"

"Yes," Kyle whispered shyly. Together they both prayed for Kyle's salvation. That day, he was saved. When they were done, Kyle smiled from ear to ear. "Can I get a new name like Paul?" Kyle asked excitedly. He felt that having a new name would be fun, and since he didn't have any paperwork or anything that contained his old name, he figured he could just choose a new one.

"I guess you can. What do you want? To be called Pyle?" the pastor chuckled.

"No!" Kyle laughed. "I want it to be somethin' cool! Maybe somethin' from the Bible?"

"Well, if you ask me, I think you share a few qualities similar to King David."

"King sounds good." Kyle smirked.

"He was a man after God's own heart, and he was very brave. You were very brave to come here today to return my Bible, and you showed that you want to please the Lord. You know, an important step in a Christian's life is being baptized. Next Sunday is the day we baptize." The pastor smiled, and Kyle nodded yes. Then David got up from the pew, thanked the pastor for everything, and headed out into the daylight.

CHAPTER 2

DAVID'S FAMILY

"So you picked the name David?" concluded the social worker once David was done explaining everything to her. He was inside his area's local foster care and adoption facility, sitting across from the social worker's desk, inside her small cubicle. David felt very cramped and very nervous inside the facility, but his heart had a new feeling of hope, which burned within him. After leaving the church that Sunday, David didn't want to go back to his shelter. It seemed to him a sad place now, filled with memories of dark nights and depressed thoughts. He now felt he had more joyful feelings inside of him than ever before. Long ago, he promised himself he would never enter a social services office again, but now seeing how Pastor Stanson, a caring adult, helped him, the idea of obeying the social services office workers was more agreeable.

The fact was that the social worker hadn't stopped typing on her computer since he came in, and after a couple of minutes of awkward silence, she finally took a break from typing and explained, "Well I'm glad you came in finally, David. As a minor, you are not allowed to be on your own."

"I know," interrupted David, rolling his eyes to signify that he already knew all she was going to say.

"Hmm, well I believe we may know of a couple looking to adopt. That is, if you are interested of course."

"For real! I'm down!" shouted David with delight. Before that day, he had always thought he was better off living his life on his own without any parents to hold him down. Seeing how Pastor Stanson had guided him, he realized that perhaps having some adults in his life that he could depend on wasn't such a bad idea after all. Then without so much as a word, the social worker stood from her desk and motioned for her colleague in the next room to come over. When he came over, together they both stared at her computer and over at David and back to the computer. They repeated this a couple times, until with a huge grin on his face, the colleague turned to the social worker and nodded yes.

"Okay then!" the lady helping David cheered, and grabbing a sticky note and a pen, she began to write down his new home address. "I'll give them a call right away. Keep this with you so you know where you are headed. I will come and escort you outside when they arrive. Now please have a seat in the waiting area," she explained as she handed him the note. Written on it was the address and David's new last name: "The residence of Mr. and Mrs. Raywood."

It was hours later when David found himself outside the social service office next to the social worker, with nothing but the small Bible the pastor had given him and eight dollars and fifty cents. Along with the clothes on his back, that was all he had to his name. He wasn't sure how his new guardians would react to his torn clothes, shaggy hair, and scarred ear, but whatever they thought, he just hoped they were kind and loving like parents should be. Within a half hour, a taxi pulled up in front of them. David eagerly peered through the car's windows the best he could, but he noticed something odd. Only the driver was inside. The social worker approached the car and asked the driver, "Are you the car the Raywoods sent?"

"Yes ma'am! Here's the address! I was sent to pick up their son? There he is! Come on lad! Ain't got all day!" the taxi driver bellowed. The social worker gave David a pat on the back and wished him well as he got into the car. He waved goodbye to her from the back seat. During the drive, David noticed new parts of town that he had never seen before. He passed residential neighborhoods, beautiful parks, and busy intersections, all the time wondering when he was going to see his new home. They passed the church on their way and David smiled. After going one block from the church, the taxi made a sharp right turn down a residential neighborhood filled with small ranch-style houses with quaint paint colors, neat lawns, and friendly smiling homeowners. Finally, amid all these pleasant houses, the taxi stopped outside a large iron and brick gate. David felt the size of the gate was completely out of place. The gate was almost as large as the homes that surrounded it.

Without any notice, the gate opened for them automatically, and the taxi pulled up a long circular, narrow driveway with a beautiful working fountain at its center. It was then that David saw what he couldn't believe, what was his new home. Towering over the taxi stood a three-story bright blue mansion. On the front, five brick steps with intricate white railing led up to a brick front porch enclosed by attractive white banisters. In the center of the porch, in front of the steps, stood a large set of grand, sophisticated oak and glass doors. Above the front porch with its own doors, held up by striking white pillars connected to the porch, was a large white balcony that stuck out from the second floor. Lining all three floors were large windows with elegantly designed frames and shutters.

David could barely breathe. He was so shocked he couldn't even exit the taxi. After a small struggle, attempting to move his trembling feet, he finally plucked up enough courage to get out of the car with the driver. For a few minutes, he stood next to the car, staring in awe at the huge house. Many different thoughts flooded his mind all at once, that he couldn't even think. Suddenly, the large oak doors opened, and a man walked out onto the front porch of the mansion. He was an older man in a tux and bowtie. His hair was thinning, and what was left of it was a light gray color. He stood as straight as a board with his hands held neatly behind his back. His eyes seemed to David to be friendly, and a smile was sitting very naturally on his face. "Hello there, young man. Your parents are waiting for you inside," the man said with a proper British accent as he motioned for David to enter through the large oak doors. David timidly began to walk up the brick front porch stairs. When he passed the man in the tux, he couldn't help but stare at him, wondering if he was somehow in a dream. The man's kind expression didn't change, and his hand remained in the same position, gesturing toward the door.

David entered through the opened doors and found himself walking into a large square open greeting area, bigger and shinier than a ballroom. The stone floor was shinier than glass, and on top was a long velvet carpet that led from the doorway straight across and up a glass spiral staircase in the center of the house. The interior of that great house was even more spectacular than the outside. The three floors of the house were stacked like a cake, with exposed hallways enclosed with white banisters similar to the ones on the front porch. On all the blue walls hung expensive paintings. Placed all around were tropical plants, rare sculptures, and valuable vases on pedestals. It was more extraordinary than David had ever imagined. As David took all of it in, he noticed standing at the foot of the spiral staircase was a middle-aged couple, arm in arm, smiling at him.

"Hello, son," said Mr. Raywood stepping forward and extending his hand out to David. Mr. Raywood's hair was black and sleek. He was dressed in a very suave suit and tie. When he extended his arm to David, David noticed a very shiny gold watch with diamonds on its face on his wrist. David timidly wiped his hand clean on his jacket and shook Mr. Raywood's hand, which felt very strong and rough.

"Oh, Jesse! How could you be so formal!" scolded his wife. She wrapped her arms around David in a big hug. She was a very thin woman with big blond hair and a sparkling red dress. She wore grand diamond jewelry that pressed against David as she hugged him.

"Now, Kyle is it?" began Mr. Raywood.

"David!" David blurted out; then speaking in a quieter voice out of embarrassment, he continued, "It's David."

"All right then, David. We will be having dinner in one hour. In the meantime, Mr. Gardien will see to it that you…?" Mr. Raywood paused and scrunched up his face as one does when one is thinking too hard.

"Freshen up!" interrupted his wife.

"Yes! Freshen up! Now, where is your luggage?" Mr. Raywood asked.

"I don't got any." David shrugged, and at that moment the man who met him at the door, Mr. Gardien, came up behind him and gestured for David to head up the stairs. Once David and Mr. Gardien were on the second floor and walking side by side, David felt very comfortable for a reason he did not know. "What do you do here?" he asked Mr. Gardien.

"I am the head butler and the only butler of this residence," Mr. Gardien said with a chuckle.

"Where's everybody else?" David asked as they suddenly stopped in front of a blue door to the left of the staircase and three doors down the hallway.

"I am the only hired hand of this house. Your parents rarely stay long here at their estate," Mr. Gardien explained as he took out a large set of keys on a ring. He instinctively put one of the keys in the keyhole and unlocked the door. Turning to David, he smiled and softly guided him into the room first. David couldn't believe his eyes. What he saw was a big blue room with more items in it than he had ever owned in his whole life. There was a real queen-size bed, a desk with a laptop, a fifty-inch TV, a brand-new video game console with tons of the latest video games, and much more. "This is your room now," the butler said. "I hope it is all to your liking. Your new clothes are on your bed, but first we must take care of that ear and that hair!" the butler said, disgusted, examining David's scarred ear. David's left ear had formed a bloody line across the top of it. At present, it was so new and red that it was impossible to ignore. In a flash, the butler exited the room and returned just as fast with a first aid kit, a comb, and a canister of hair gel. "Now hold still," Mr. Gardien urged, pressing a cotton ball to David's ear.

"Ow!" David exclaimed and twitched.

"I apologize, but it has to be sanitized! Now let us address this hair. It is much too long to be taken seriously!" Mr. Gardien scoffed as he pulled out a pair of scissors from the desk drawer. David had never had a haircut before, that he could remember anyway, and before he knew it, the butler was behind him, trimming off his long black locks. Clip after clip, David's long greasy hair fell to the floor, and he actually felt a bit cleaner, but what remained was still greasy. So Mr. Gardien led David to the house bathroom and handed him a blue robe. "I have run you a bath. Freshen up! Once you are finished, go to your room and dress for dinner. I will come to your room and check on you to see if you require any further assistance as soon as I have finished preparing your dinner," the butler said, closing the bathroom door behind him. David took his bath with immense enjoyment. It was the kind of pleasure that is hard to describe. To put it plainly, this was the first bath he had had in many months, and it felt amazing. He never wanted it to end. However, his stomach growled in protest, and after a half hour, he exited the bath in his robe and walked down the hall to his new room. Fifteen minutes later, a soft knock was heard at David's door. "Master David, your dinner is set. Are you about finished getting dressed?" Mr. Gardien called from the hallway.

"Uh, I'm confused? I need some help," David said in a puzzled tone.

"May I enter?"

"Yeah," David called, and Mr. Gardien opened the door to find David dressed in his white button-up shirt, fancy belt, black dress pants, and shoes and staring at one article of clothing in his hands that he had never seen before. "What's this?" he asked, handing it to Mr. Gardien.

"Your attire for this evening is a three-piece suit, Master David. What you are holding is your waistcoat. It goes on like so." Mr. Gardien put the vest on David and buttoned up the front of it. The waistcoat was as black as coal and matched with the black jacket that Mr. Gardien also put on David directly afterward. "There now, you're…" Mr. Gardien paused staring at David's chest. "Where is your cravat?" he shouted.

"My what?"

"Your necktie!" Mr. Gardien sighed, quickly searching the room for the missing necktie.

"Oh, it's over there. I didn't know how it went." David pointed to the tie on the floor, embarrassed. He had never learned how to tie a tie before. Mr. Gardien found the crimson necktie and went over to David. He swiftly tied the tie around David's neck and tucked it under his waistcoat.

"There, no harm done. I will teach you how to tie one on your own another time." The butler smiled. "However, presently I must finish with your hair," he said, grabbing the comb and hair gel he had left in the room before David had taken his bath. He took the comb and parted David's hair in the center so wide that a truck could drive between the sides of his hair. Speedily, he took the hair gel and slicked David's hair flat onto his head. "You look smashing!" Mr. Gardien exclaimed.

David went over to a large oval standing full-body mirror that sat next to his dresser and looked at himself. He couldn't even recognize the boy now staring back at him through the mirror. The only thing that still remained of his past was the red scar that brightly shone from his left ear. "Come along, Master David; we must join your parents at once," Mr. Gardien called from the doorway.

"Okay," David whispered, and he joined the butler in the doorway. Both of them walked downstairs to the greeting area. Across from the greeting area to the right, there were three doors. Standing amid the blue walls were two parallel doors that seemed to be the same design as the front doors and about the same size. The third door, which was a smaller swinging door one might find in a diner, had a small circular window on its face and stood very close to the parallel doors.

"That is the entrance to the kitchen"—Mr. Gardien pointed toward the swinging door—"and here is the dining hall, Master David." With that, Mr. Gardien pushed open the parallel doors just as David followed in behind him. Mr. and Mrs. Raywood were already present, seated at the far end of an extremely long table. The elegant table and chairs were the only pieces of furniture in that spacious hall. Above the table hung a grand, awe-inspiring chandelier lit with thousands of candles. On the table sat pure gold and silver plates of every different size filled with side dishes from around the world. In the center sat a full oven-roasted turkey, baked ham, roasted chicken, grilled salmon, and sautéed vegetarian pasta, all resting on individual raised silver platters alongside their individual cloches for covering. It was more food than anyone could eat in one sitting. As David walked into the room, his parents stood to greet him.

"You look adorable!" Mrs. Raywood cheered.

"Very sophisticated!" Mr. Raywood complimented in a pleased tone.

"Thank you," David muttered standing in the doorway, looking around in amazement. "Are we having a party?" he asked, staring at the food.

"No, silly, come sit down. We were unsure as to what your food preferences are, so we decided to have everything," Mrs. Raywood chuckled. David took a seat to the left of his father, who sat at the head of the table, and across from his mother, who sat to the right of his father. He was about to grab at the bowl of caviar to see what it was, when his father extended his hand to him. His mother did the same, and they all three held hands, bowed their heads, and prayed. Mr. and Mrs. Raywood thanked the Lord for bringing them David, and for blessing them so abundantly. Once they had finished, David began filling his plate to the limit. Manners wise, he was very unfamiliar, but his parents didn't mind seeing this was his first time, in a long time, eating at an actual table. In the middle of stuffing his face full of turkey and chicken, David looked up and noticed Mr. Gardien standing in the corner of the room, watching them eat.

"Maybe he doesn't feel well?" David concluded, while trying to fit a whole bowl full of lobster bisque into his mouth and seeing that Mr. Gardien had not joined them for dinner. When he was finally full and could eat no more, he lounged back in his chair and let out a big burp.

"Excuse you, young man." His father chuckled.

"Oh, sorry," David said, trying to undo his waistcoat. That moment was the fullest he had been in his entire life.

"David, we have something very important to discuss with you," his father explained in a serious tone, taking his mother's hand and sharing a nervous smile with her. David gave them his full attention. "You see, son, you are a part of this family now. You do want to be, I presume?"

"Uh-huh!"

"Good," his father chuckled, quickly returning to his serious tone. "Being our son means you inherit all that is before you. What is ours is yours now, and that comes with a lot of responsibility. You see, what your mother and I do for a living is we both run a company that helps make contracts between international corporations and companies. We help them navigate through other countries' laws, understand cultural differences, and break through the language barrier by translating legal terms and so forth. And in order for us to do our jobs and keep the company running, we both have to travel very extensively."

His mother chimed in. "What your father is trying to say, David, is we aren't home in the country often."

"But you guys'll be around sometimes, right? You can't be working all the time?"

The couple's faces were downcast. Mr. Raywood put his hand onto David's shoulder. "This is where responsibility plays a hand, my dear boy. Your mother and I will be lucky if we get any holidays off, let alone weekends. Mr. Gardien will be here to assist you in the day-to-day operations of the household. He will be in charge of your financial affairs while we are away. He is your trustee until you are of age."

"So I won't ever get to see you?"

"Oh no, dear!" his mother cried, standing from her chair and heading over to hug him. "We will have our phones. You can call us and message us, and we even have video phone calling now!"

"But I don't got a phone," David protested.

"Oh, well we should remedy that straight away! Will this do?" his father smiled, signaling Mr. Gardien to come closer to the table. Mr. Gardien came quickly over to David and presented him with a small blue box with a green ribbon wrapped around it. "Think of this as your welcome home gift." His father laughed as David tore into the wrapping as if it were his first ever gift. Once the gift wrap was removed and the box opened, David could see it was a new touch-screen phone with new wireless headphones.

"It is the latest model," his mother added. "With a beautiful black case that I chose for you," she said proudly. David was speechless. He finally had a phone of his very own. A tear came into view as he hugged both of his parents and thanked them heavily.

The next morning David was awoken by a knock at his door. "Master David! It's morning!" called Mr. Gardien cheerily.

"So?" mumbled David in response, pulling his sports-themed blankets over his head. He wasn't a morning person.

"Time to get up! Work to be done! Your parents have already left for their flight! They had to be in France early this morning! Take your bath and come downstairs at once!" the butler bellowed and left. David hated getting up early and was planning on ignoring the butler's wake-up call when he smelled the scent of bacon cooking.

"Yum!" he cheered, jumping out of bed and grabbing his blue robe. He ran to the bathroom and jumped into the bath that Mr. Gardien had prepared him. After his bath, he headed downstairs in his robe. "Good morning!" David yelled, running to the dining table. Mr. Gardien set a plate before him with two big waffles and two sticks of bacon.

"Good morning, Master David!" the butler said sunnily.

"Uh, Mr. Gardien? Please don't call me master. It's weird, man."

"All right, how would you wish me to address you then?"

David laughed. "Just David, dude."

"Fine, David it is. And since we are on the subject of name-calling, you may address me as Mister, or Mr. Gardien. Never 'man' or 'dude.' Do I make myself clear?" Mr. Gardien said gravely.

David gave a mischievous smile, and with a laugh he teased, "You got it, G! Whatever you say, homie! G-man! Hey! How 'bout 'G-man'! It can be your rapper name!" David busted up laughing.

Mr. Gardien, in that moment, gave a mischievous smile of his own and responded, "If you address me as G-man, then I have the right to address you as little duckie," he said, rubbing David's hair mockingly.

"Hey! Watch the hair! I just got all that sticky junk out! What kinda name is duckie, anyway?"

"That's what my mum used to call me." Mr. Gardien sighed, standing behind David, daydreaming. A few silent and awkward moments went by as Mr. Gardien daydreamed about his childhood and David finished his breakfast.

"There's another thing," David said, picking up his last piece of bacon.

"Yes, how may I be of service?" recited the butler snapping out of his dream.

"Don't you ever eat?"

"Of course I do?"

"Why don't you eat with me?"

"Oh no!" Mr. Gardien laughed. "A gentlemen's gentlemen does not dine with his employer. He dines once his employer is finished. Now enough chitchat, we have pressing business to attend to!" Mr. Gardien said, taking David's plate away.

"But! I don't—"

"No buts! Presently, I called the local junior high school, and we resolved that they will permit you to begin school in the seventh grade, where you are supposed to be. However, as a result of you not attending sixth grade, they insist you have a tutor to help you measure up. I will have no debate on the matter! You will attend school, am I clear?"

"Okay. I ain't got anything else to do," David shrugged. The night before, he had prayed to the Lord, like he saw the pastor and his father do, and he asked the Lord to show him what He wanted him to do. The Lord, through His Holy Spirit, put it on David's heart to be obedient to Mr. Gardien, and he was going to do it.

"You're just going to obey me? No fuss?" the butler gasped, confused.

"Sure," David said, sipping his milk. "I asked the Lord to give me a family who loves me, and He has! The least I could do is listen to you. So when do I start?"

"Today."

David choked on his milk. "Today!" he yelled.

"Yes, today is Monday, Mast—" Mr. Gardien hadn't time to finish. David threw down his cup and ran upstairs to his room.

"I can't go in my robe!" he yelled, running over to his closet. He flung his closet door open and found hundreds of outfits all neatly pressed and hung with plastic coverings on them. Each outfit had a little label on it. "Swim wear," "party suit," "golfing outfit," "evening suit," "dancing suit," and "sleep wear" were just a few of the outfits he passed through. "Ain't there somethin' normal?" he said out loud in frustration. At last he found what he had in mind, an outfit consisting of a pair of blue jeans and a black T-shirt labeled "work clothes."

"School's work." David shrugged as he pulled the plastic off the clothes and quickly put them on. Then he looked at himself in his oval mirror. His hair still had a little hair gel left in it from the night before, and it was a mess. "I ain't got time for this!" David said, running his hands through his hair. He moved his hands back and forth and all around until he made his hair look like a wave in the ocean, with spikes like mountains in the front and a curve in the back. "I like that! I look fly!" David said, checking his new hairstyle in the mirror. He turned around and searched for the suit he had worn the night before. He found it piled up on the floor on top of his black dress shoes, and he grabbed for his shoes with gusto. He put on his shoes and socks as fast as he could and headed out of his room. Mr. Gardien was outside in the hallway, sweeping the floor, waiting to greet David.

When he saw what David had on, he gave a look of terror. "Your parents would have me thrown out in the London fog if they saw you attend school in that! As your legal guardian, I demand you dress in your formal apparel at once!"

"No way! Get real! Everyone'll laugh at me! I got a right to pick my own clothes!"

"Well, it seems we are at an impasse," Mr. Gardien said, crossing his arms. "You will not pass without changing," he commanded, blocking David's path.

"Oh yeah!" David yelled; he turned and the first thing he saw was a lavish painting of two men fencing that hung next to his door. He looked down and noticed a smaller broom sitting next to his room's door. He grabbed it and held the broom handle out like a sword. "I dare you to a sword fight! I win, I go like this. You win, I'll…" David paused and thought for a moment. "I'll put on one part of the suit!"

"I believe you mean broom fight? I do not have to duel; you will do as I say, and besides this is childish!" Mr. Gardien protested. David hit Mr. Gardien's broom handle with his, making the broom fall from the butler's hand. Mr. Gardien's expression became all the more serious. He held his head high as he bent to pick up his broom. Then without a word, Mr. Gardien got into a fencing position and shouted, "On guard!" The duel was on, broom handles were flying, the combatants were laughing, and they both gave each other quite a challenge. Finally, in the end Mr. Gardien gave a finishing poke to David's stomach. "That's game," the butler said, breathing heavy. "Now I believe some promises were made. I do recall that if I won, you were to put on your suit?"

"One piece from the suit!"

"All right, if that is the best we can do. Just make sure it is an actual piece of your suit and not your belt or something silly." Next moment, David came out in his black T-shirt, jeans, and dress shoes and sporting his coal black waistcoat over it all.

"Ta da!" he said proudly. "Cool, huh?"

"Yes, yes. Now come along! We mustn't be late for your first day!" Mr. Gardien said, handing David his new fully packed, stylish blue backpack. Mr. Gardien led David out to the Raywoods' ginormous garage. It was filled with several different expensive vintage and famous cars, one of which was a long and luxurious black limousine.

"Are we takin' the limo!" David grinned, peering in its windows.

"No, no. Taking you to school is one of my chores, so we will take my car," the butler said, proudly removing a sheet and uncovering an old four-door jalopy. Mr. Gardien whistled and exclaimed, "Ain't she a beaut!" The butler glowed with pride. David questioned if it would even start. It did, and soon they were off to David's first day of school.

CHAPTER 3

SOMEBODY ELSE'S STORY

The old jalopy happily chugged down the road. David looked excitedly out the back-seat window. They had passed the church a few turns back, and David enjoyed seeing all the different street names and places he had never seen before. Soon they came to a large sign that read "Lancer Middle School," and Mr. Gardien pulled into the student drop-off zone. The jalopy stopped right in the front of the school, and David stepped out. "Make sure to pick up your class schedule from the front office!" Mr. Gardien told him before he closed the door.

"Got it, G-man!" David smiled.

"Have fun, little duck!" the butler shouted out the window as he drove away. As David turned around, he suddenly found himself alone, staring at a large school filled with teenagers like him. It was quite bewildering for David, who had never seen so many teens in one place. About a hundred students stood around on their phones, waiting for the day to start. He looked around and saw that the school was an outdoor campus, with gray pillars that held up concrete slabs that covered the students from the sun, snow, and rain. On each end of the concrete slabs, there were many long, narrow buildings lined with doors. In the center of the concrete courtyard, there were iron lunch tables held together by chains, and next to the lunch tables stood a small brown one-story building with three extremely wide and long concrete stairs that encircled the building all around. Next to this building, there was a small sign on a stick that read "Library" in cursive letters. David looked to his right and saw two other large distinct buildings. One building was very tall and very wide and had two large parallel doors at its entrance, and above these doors, a small sign had written on it the word "cafeteria." Next to the cafeteria was a smaller and thinner building with glass windows and doors that also had a sign. This building's sign read, "Office." So David thought it a good idea to go inside that building to retrieve his new schedule.

When he came back out with his new schedule in hand, he stared steadily at the words on the paper, trying to make sense of the names and numbers that were written on it. He looked up and saw many more students filling the outside halls, sitting at the lunch tables, and crowding every available space. A loneliness crept into his heart as he watched them all smile and laugh together, texting each other and listening to each other's headphones. He was on an island separated from the fun. A fear crept into his heart, a fear of having to talk and interrupt these happy people, and a fear of standing out.

He was busy wondering what he could say to make himself sound cool when a familiar voice broke his wondering. "Hi there! I remember you!" a cheerful girl's voice shouted amid the crowds. As she was running full speed toward him, David saw the curly red-haired girl that had greeted him the day before at the church. She had on a green dress this time, with black stockings and brown boots.

"Church girl!" he said in surprise once she had made it over to him. She paused for a moment to catch her breath and fix her boot. Another girl had followed close behind her. The other girl wore a modest pink blouse and blue jeans. She had on zero makeup, and on her feet, she wore bright pink athletic running shoes. Her hair was bright golden blond, and it crowned her soft alabaster face. As it blew in the autumn breeze, David thought she was very pretty, but what attracted him more was her kind smile. Somehow, he felt she had a kind heart, and this made him want to know more about her and get to know her.

In that moment, he was distracted by her gentle smile until the red-haired girl spoke up. "You came to my church! Pastor Stanson was so happy to meet you! Are you coming next Sunday? Next Sunday is baptism Sunday and…" She noticed he wasn't listening and saw his focus was only on her friend. "Oh, where are my manners! My name is Moriah." The red-haired girl continued, shaking David's hand to bring him out of his trance. "And this is Abigail," she said, pointing to her blond friend.

"Hey," David whispered shyly, waving to Abigail though she was only a few feet in front of him.

"So you're new here, huh? Don't worry one bit! We can show you around! Come on!" Moriah said, taking David's schedule out of his hand and tugging him by the arm, leading him through the crowds. Abigail followed on David's other side, and soon they were all three walking down the hallway together. Though it would have been hard for David to believe that Moriah wasn't always as cheerful as she was then, the truth was she had just recently become this way. A month ago, something happened that changed how she viewed her entire life, and it all started at lunch. Moriah normally sat alone during lunchtime at school because she didn't fit in well with the other teens. She was saved and baptized at age ten, and she always tried to obey the Lord and His Word, which wasn't looked upon favorably at her school. She didn't have many peers in her life that she could call friends. Most were merely acquaintances. So that she wouldn't feel like a loner, sitting by herself at a cafeteria table, she enjoyed having her lunch sitting on the school's soccer field bleachers, feeding the birds the extra crust she had torn off of her peanut butter and jelly sandwiches. One day, as she had just finished her lunch and was about to begin reading a special book about a lion and four kids, Valery, the coolest girl in school, along with her six copycat friends came over. Valery was the kind of girl who only cares about what a person is wearing, rather than who they are on the inside. She could be mean to anyone who was not as fashionable as she was, and that was pretty much every other girl in school besides her six friends. Valery had long black flowing hair, and she wore tons of makeup, enough makeup for three girls. She always dressed in her favorite skintight black turtleneck sweater with different extremely short skirts. Adding some stylish belts and matching shoes always completed her fitted outfit. Her six friends all made sure they were on Valery's good side by dressing exactly like her. They all had black hair, tons of makeup on, and articles of black clothing that they wore every day. The only person in school that Valery felt was fashionable without black hair, black clothes, and a lot of makeup was Moriah. Moriah always had on nice blouses and modest dresses. She also wore makeup, though not as much as Valery and her gang, and her red hair was always blowing in the wind as beautiful as a sunset at the peak of dawn. The fact that Valery knew how pretty Moriah was made Valery all the more meaner to her for it. If Valery had the chance to hurt Moriah's feelings, she would take it in a heartbeat. Today was that opportunity. As Valery approached Moriah on the bleachers, Moriah pretended to be wrapped up in her book, but this didn't stop Valery from making the first comment.

"Hey! This isn't a library!" Valery scoffed as her clique came tracing behind her.

"I am shocked you know what a library even looks like, Valery," moaned Moriah, who was used to these kinds of dealings with Valery. "I have just as much right to be here as you do."

"We need a new place to eat lunch, and we want to eat here!" Valery demanded as her gang all shook their heads in agreement.

"You can have the whole rest of the bleachers, Valery. I just want to finish this chapter, and I will be out of your way."

"Fine! Have it your way." Valery shrugged. She and her gang climbed up and over Moriah to the left side of the bleachers. They all finished their lunches and talked about the latest news about boys and gossip. It was about halfway through lunch when Valery turned her attention back to Moriah, who was still busy reading her book quietly. "Hey, Moriah, do you have a Face-novel?" Valery yelled down to her.

"Huh? What?" Moriah said, coming out of her book.

"You know, Face-novel? Instant Photograph? On your phone, book head!" Valery bellowed.

"Oh, I don't have those," Moriah said sadly. Her parents didn't believe a teenager her age should have a social media account until they were at least sixteen, and Moriah was only thirteen.

"Of course you don't. You never do anything cool." Valery laughed, and her clique all joined in.

"I bet your user profile would have like zero followers. Hashtag loser!" one of Valery's friends, whose eyes never left her phone, said, and the girls all laughed again.

"You're such a nerd! The only reason you read all those books is 'cause you don't have any real friends," the gossip of Valery's friends chimed in. Moriah didn't have a word to say. Sure, afterward she could think of many good things to respond, but at the time she sat speechless with her mouth open wide for what seemed like hours; in truth it was only a moment.

Valery began again. "You're so weird. I bet you don't even have a phone."

"Yes, I do!" Moriah yelled, taking out her touch-screen phone and showing it to them.

"So, why don't you have any accounts?" Valery asked, honestly confused.

"My parents won't let me."

"Oh, well when you can make your own decisions, then maybe I'll let you join my Instant Photograph," Valery scoffed with a wave of her night black hair. "Come on, guys. Let's go find some cute boys to talk to." With that, Valery and her followers all got up and walked away, leaving their words like knives in Moriah's heart. She sat on the bleachers the rest of lunch, trying to make sense of what happened.

The girls' words flooded her mind like an ocean. "What do they mean? I'm not a nerd! I'm just not allowed to have those kinds of things yet," she thought, trying to justify herself against their words. She unknowingly allowed their words to become a standard by which she judged her worth. Not wanting to call herself a nerd, by their standard, she subconsciously decided her scapegoat would be her parents. "It's their fault! Them telling me I cannot have a social media account until I'm sixteen or whatever," she thought angrily. "Well fine! I'll ask them if I can have some accounts, and then I'll be cool!"

Moriah walked home that day very glum and very lost in thought. Her tan ranch-style house looked somewhat gloomier than usual, which normally is what happens when one is sad. Moriah knew her home and her family better than anyone. She had been homeschooled from kindergarten to sixth grade and had recently been enrolled in public school because her mother had accepted a full-time job to help with the finances. Moriah's house was right next to the church that her family attended and her father worked at. Moriah's father was hired as the church's head ministry administrator. This meant that her father spent many days and nights hard at work attempting to form missionary teams and get funding to go on mission trips.

Unofficially, however, he also spent much time filling out church paperwork, fixing problems, and handling disagreements within the congregation. In fact, he spent so much time at the church fixing things that some new members of the congregation started mistakenly calling him pastor. Her dad's workload always seemed like a lot to Moriah, who grew up in the church. She was always busy helping her parents with anything that needed to be done for the church. Everyone in the congregation knew her name and had helped to raise her and her siblings at some point or another. They all knew about Moriah's life and her sibling's lives like they were family. She went to youth group every Wednesday, church every Sunday, and Bible study every Thursday, and she volunteered at every single church event throughout the year.

She was the middle child of the family, in between her eighteen-year-old sister, Michaela, and her three-year-old baby sister, Mabel. Michaela had just started college at the beginning of fall and was living on campus in the dorms. Moriah missed her terribly. They were very close growing up. Being homeschooled together, they always found time to play together and to share stories as only sisters can.

Later that evening, as Moriah sat down to dinner with her parents and Mabel, she thought hard about what was the best way to bring up that she wanted a social media account. Her mother prayed, and when she was done, they all dug into her mother's homemade stew. "So how was school today, sweetheart?" her mother asked, like she did every evening since Moriah started attending public school.

"I had another run-in with Valery today," Moriah said sadly, putting down her fork.

"What kind of run-in?" her mother asked concernedly.

"We said if she spoke meanly to you one more time, the principal was to hear from me. They need to reform their bullying policy!" her father added.

"She keeps saying rude things to me. I try to ignore her, but that doesn't work."

"I'll have a talk with your principal tomorrow after I talk with the roofing company about fixing that hole in the church's nursery ceiling. In the meantime, have you tried showing her kindness? That might work. We are supposed to love our enemies you know," her father said in a lecturing tone, quoting scripture.

Moriah rolled her eyes. "You just don't understand," she mumbled under her breath, pushing her plate away. A moment went by; then Moriah spoke in a louder tone. "Uh, Mom? Dad? Can I ask you something?" she said anxiously.

"Sure, sweetie, what is it?" her mother replied.

"Can I have a social media account? All the other girls have one, and I'm the only one without one!"

"I'm sure you're not the only one without one. You know the rules, not until you are sixteen," her father said in between spoonfuls of stew.

"You know, dear, we had a similar conversation with your sister when she was your age. Back then, she wasn't allowed to have a phone until she was sixteen. You already have a phone; you should be grateful," her mother said in a soothing tone.

"I am grateful for what I have! Since I'm able to have a phone younger, why can't I have an account?"

"Young people your age are known to be irresponsible on those things. We are just trying to protect you, honey," her father said, finishing his stew.

"You're impossible!" Moriah yelled out; she was frustrated and overwhelmed with her parents' lack of compromise. "You never let me do anything!"

"Watch your tone, young lady! Remember, honor your father and mother," her father said, quoting scripture. Moriah felt unheard and misunderstood. Her heart sank not only because she wasn't going to be allowed a social media account but also because she felt her parents simply were not listening to her. In a huff, she got up, ran through the house into her room, and slammed the door.

She threw herself onto her bed and started to think out loud. "Why does he always do that? Why does he use the Bible against me?" Her eyes slowly began to scan her room. All around hung medals from Bible-verse-memorizing competitions and church game participation from when she was young. Also from her childhood hung photos of her at VBS, church picnics, church plays, church parties, church carnivals, and many other church events and programs.

Instead of the honor she normally felt when she stared at these pictures and awards, she suddenly felt even sadder than before. "Why should I show Valery any kindness? She is never kind to me! Why does the Lord want me to love my enemies? That makes no sense!" she thought out loud. She paused and looked up at her wall of family photos. Rapidly, she got off her bed and took one framed photo down from her wall. It was a photo of her family from last Christmas. Her mother and father behind her, her older sister and her baby sister on either side of her, and her in the middle. They were all standing in front of their family Christmas tree, dressed in matching sweaters. Moriah focused in on her older sister in the photo. Her sister's face was happy and smiley. Thinking about her sister living two hours or more away from home made Moriah's heart even sadder. A gloomy expression came over Moriah's face. She put the photo down and got out her purple school backpack. She reached in and took out her Bible that she carried around with her everywhere she went. She stared hard at the Bible. She knew every book name in the Bible in order. She knew at least one hundred verses from memory, and she knew much theology about the Bible as a whole, from going to church every Sunday of her life. However, for the first time, she really doubted if she really believed in the Bible this time. Though she tried, she couldn't feel the Lord with her. Her heart ached from what Valery had said to her, and showing them any kindness seemed way too hard. "I know I should have faith," she said out loud. "But how? Why? When? Heh, I am starting to sound like Investigator Jane." Investigator Jane was Moriah's favorite mystery novel series. The series was about a fictional teenage girl detective who solved crimes around her neighborhood. "I know! I will be like Investigator Jane!" Moriah said, turning around to find her limited-edition Investigator Jane detective hat and magnifying glass.

On the opposite side of her room stood two child-size bookshelves filled with some of her favorite books. The top shelves of these bookshelves were reserved solely for her Investigator Jane collector's edition book series. Over these bookshelves were two giant author-signed Investigator Jane movie posters, and on top of the bookshelves sat all of

Moriah's Investigator Jane memorabilia. Her Investigator Jane replica pink plaid detective jacket, limited-edition pink plaid detective hat, and her limited-edition signed replica magnifying glass all sat neatly organized. She quickly put on her hat and grabbed her magnifying glass. "All right, Bible! You're going under the radar!" she said in a deep voice, imitating Investigator Jane. Pointing her magnifying glass at her Bible, she repeated Investigator Jane's famous catchphrase: "I'm going to find your motive, your past, and your secrets!"

The next day, Moriah skipped into her school's small brown library. Moriah's favorite place to relax was the library. When she was being homeschooled by her mom, she had every Monday off from schoolwork, and Moriah always wanted to go hang out at their local public library. She loved reading, and she loved books, and since she wanted to find out more about the Bible, she figured the best place to start was her school's library. "Excuse me," Moriah said sweetly to the librarian on duty. "Where would the theology section be?"

"In a private school," the librarian answered crossly. "We don't have those books here. Maybe try the science section." Moriah's eyes widened. She didn't expect such a harsh reply.

"Thank you," she said shyly as she exited the library. "Now where do I go?" she wondered as she walked over to the cafeteria lunch line to buy lunch. "Maybe my sister's school has a theology section?" she pondered. So she got out her phone and began texting her sister. The next day was a Saturday, but it wasn't any ordinary Saturday for Moriah. The next day was Sister Saturday, the one Saturday a month when Michaela would drive home and pick up Moriah and Mabel in her little car and hang out with them all day and have dinner at home.

"Here we go, my school's main library," Michaela said as she led Moriah and Mabel through the front doors of her college's giant two-story library. Moriah walked in with her mouth open wide. She was in awe. She had never seen so many books. Michaela laughed at her sister's expression, and picking up Mabel in her arms, she explained, "Okay, I got a paper due that I haven't even started on, so I'm gonna grab some coffee and work on it outside at the tables. Don't worry about Mabel; she's with me and she has her dolls. Text me when you're done."

With that, Moriah's sisters left, and Moriah felt very nervous. She had never been on a college campus before, and she had never been inside such a big library. However, her determination got the better of her, and she decided to look into the library database for what she wanted. She had been in enough libraries to know how to navigate one, even one of this size. She found the library database on one of the library's computers, and she found the section number she needed. After that, she wandered and wandered until finally she found what she was looking for, the theology section. "Time to investigate!" she said, imitating her favorite detective once again.

Once inside the section, she got to work. She found dictionaries, encyclopedias, and maps dedicated to things about the Bible. She found board-reviewed and peer-reviewed articles inside of accredited journals. She found novels and textbooks written by famous authors with doctorate and master's degrees. She found research from experts in their respected fields and by scientists and accredited pastors. She taught herself how to use some of the Bible concordances, and she even found some books that were written completely in Hebrew and Greek. She looked up many definitions and explanations of various words and passages she had heard throughout her life. She even found out about archaeologists and their findings about places and things that occurred in the Bible. When she was done, she had three entire composition notebooks filled with information she had gathered about Jesus, the Bible, and its history, and there were still many more books and much more information that she hadn't even touched yet. Throughout all her research, she made sure to only trust the sources that lined up and agreed with the Bible. This information about the Bible was evidence she had found from partial and impartial sources that no one could dispute as unscholarly, but Moriah knew that just because something is scholarly doesn't automatically make it true. She knew she had to accept that the Bible was true in her heart. However, she still found herself wrestling with doubt inside her heart. It felt like her mind was satisfied with believing in the Bible, but her heart wasn't fully there yet. She suddenly reached into her purple backpack and pulled out her worn, sparkly purple locked diary that she had kept since she was a child. Every day around her neck, she always wore a small child-size cross from when she was very young, and on her wrist she always wore the same charm bracelet that she and her sister made when they were children. On this bracelet, she secretly kept the key to her secret diary. She carefully found the key and unlocked her diary. She grabbed a pencil and wrote the date and where she was in the library.

She began her entry like she always did by writing, "Dear Diary." Then she wrote down her thoughts: "I don't feel God's presence, and I've been sad a lot. I found sources today that show me that having faith doesn't mean throwing away logic and reason. A bunch of smart people believe in the Bible, but I'm still not sure. God's Word has to be my ultimate source of Truth. I'm still struggling with doubt. Do my doubts mean I'm not a follower of Christ? Do they mean I don't love God?"

Moriah signed her full name, Moriah MacAaron, at the bottom of her diary entry and exited the library.

When she came out of the library, she saw Michaela sitting at a table, typing furiously on her laptop, and enjoying a cup of vanilla ice cream. Next to her sat Mabel in her car seat on a chair, playing with her dolls and covered in chocolate ice cream. Moriah came out gloomily and took a seat next to them. Michaela slid a cup of strawberry ice cream toward her, Moriah's favorite. Moriah ate it slowly, completely lost in thought. "Did you find what you were looking for?" Michaela asked with a concerned expression on her face.

Moriah snapped out of her thoughts and realized she hadn't spoken. "Oh, yeah. Thank you for the ice cream. I found out a lot about the Bible. I found out it didn't just fall out of the sky one day." Moriah laughed awkwardly.

A pause went by; then Mabel asked softly, "Moriah? Do you love us anymore?" Moriah gave a shocked expression. She loved her sisters very deeply; that's why Mabel's question hurt her very much.

"Of course I do! Why would you ask something like that?"

"'Cause you ran away from Mommy and Daddy," Mabel said, continuing to play with her dolls.

"What's she talking about, little sis?" Michaela asked Moriah. Moriah looked down at her feet. She didn't want to admit to her sister that she had fought with their parents because she was ashamed of her behavior.

"Dad and I just had a little disagreement last Thursday night," Moriah mumbled.

Michaela laughed. "Like that time, remember in the middle of the school year, we went to the beach for a week, and when we got back, Mom had us do extra work to make up for the time we lost. You were so mad!"

Moriah hated that memory, so she gave Michaela an angry look and scoffed. "No, not like that time!" Then she turned her focus back to Mabel. "Mabel, of course I still love you and Mommy and Daddy and Michaela. Sometimes I get angry, but just because sometimes I don't feel like it, doesn't mean I don't love my family. Love isn't just a feeling; it's more than that."

Suddenly, Moriah understood one of the answers to her questions. She quickly got out her diary and opened it with her key. "You still wear our old charm bracelet? And you still carry around that worn-out book? It's like eight years old!" Michaela teased.

"So?" Moriah protested.

Michaela laughed. "It's older than Mabel!"

"Most things are older than Mabel; she's only three!" Moriah and her sister laughed. As they laughed, Moriah took out a pencil, and she wrote down her realization. "Love, real love, is more than a feeling. Faith is more than a feeling too. So even though I don't feel God's presence, I still have faith that He is God." With that, Moriah closed her diary and finished eating her ice cream and hanging out with her sisters.

When Moriah and her sisters came home in through the door that Saturday evening, her parents were hard at work setting up their weekly family game night. Her mother was busy making popcorn in the kitchen, and her father was attempting to pick up all the spilled board game pieces that he had dropped. "We've been waiting for you girls. How was Michaela's college, Moriah?" her father asked, standing to his feet.

"Fine, I found out a lot about Jesus and scripture," she said in a small voice. Michaela took this as an opportunity to take Mabel to put away her dolls and exited the room with Mabel. Then in an even shier tone, Moriah whispered, "Uh, Dad? I'm sorry for Thursday night. I was frustrated and—"

"It's all right, honey. I know school is a hard time for you right now," her father interrupted.

"But it wasn't just school. I..." Moriah paused, unable to find the right words to say.

"You got upset because I quoted a verse you didn't want to hear," her father said, finishing her sentence. "But there are a lot of verses in scripture that people don't want to hear, honey. But that doesn't make them any less God's Word."

"I know, I found that out today, that the Bible didn't just fall out of the sky one day. But, Dad, do my doubts mean I'm no longer God's child?"

Warmly her father slowly smiled, and he placed his hand on Moriah's shoulder. "Moriah, an important strategy, when it comes to doubt, is to not give up. God's grace is sufficient for you. He knows your heart.

He knows everything about you, even the parts you wish to hide from Him. Take heart, His grace is enough for you and your doubts. I mean, doubting Thomas isn't called doubting Thomas for no reason, and he was a disciple. No, Moriah, your doubts do not mean you are no longer God's child. Hopefully, they will serve to make you stronger in your faith." Moriah hadn't thought about that before. Talking about her doubts and finally telling another Godly person she had them made her heart feel lighter. After that, Moriah's faith was strengthened, and after a while her doubts slowly diminished. In that moment, she embraced her father and thanked him.

"What's going on in here, you two?" her mother asked, bringing in the popcorn.

"Our daughter has become a theologian," her father laughed. "I'm so proud!"

"Dad!" Moriah moaned. Then, she made a face as if she remembered something she had forgotten. "Oh, and Mom! Dad! Having a social media account doesn't seem as important to me anymore. In fact, what those girls said about me doesn't seem as important to me anymore, because Michaela and I were talking about stuff you always told us growing up and I realized something today."

"And what's that?" her mother asked.

"That since God's Word is true, then what He says about me is true. That means that I'm fearfully and wonderfully made, like you always tell me."

"That's the truth, dear; you know it is." Her father smiled warmly. The rest of the night, Moriah's family all gathered around their favorite board game table and enjoyed their family game night.

The next morning, Sunday, Moriah prayed to the Lord and asked Him to have His will be done in her life and to create in her a renewed heart. The Lord did so, and His spirit stirred within her. That morning, Moriah thought about her father's advice more practically. "It is true that Jesus commands me to love my enemies," she said out loud, "and I can for sure call Valery my enemy!" She laughed. Showing kindness to Valery did seem more doable once Moriah remembered how Jesus loves her even though she, herself, doesn't deserve it. She also thought about how Jesus loves Valery and wants Valery to be saved too. She concluded that since Jesus commands His followers to love their enemies, that must mean that doing what He commands is what is best. Moriah wanted to obey God's commands because she loved Him, but she wasn't sure how to show Valery kindness. That Sunday, Pastor Stanson preached a sermon on forgiveness and challenged the congregation to invite some of their friends and coworkers to church next Sunday for free donuts and coffee. After that, Moriah knew what she was going to do. She knew Jesus would help her to do it, and that Sunday she made up a plan.

The next day, Monday, Moriah intentionally walked over to her favorite lunch spot at lunchtime. Sure enough, Valery and her clique were sitting in Moriah's favorite spot on the bleachers, throwing their trash onto the soccer field. Moriah straightened her glasses, brushed off her dress, and marched right up to Valery and her friends. "Well, if it isn't the book nerd," Valery sneered. "Why don't you go sit by yourself; you're good at that." She laughed along with her clique.

"You know what else I'm good at, Valery? Research. I found out Saturday from a bunch of scholarly sources that the Bible is a reliable source. Not only that, but the Bible claims it's God's Word, and I know it is. It is my source of Truth, and inside, it tells of the greatest love story ever told! God sent His son to pay for our sins by dying on the cross." At this Moriah showed Valery her little cross necklace. "God's Son is named Jesus Christ, and He is my Savior. He can be yours too. My church has a thing called youth group every Wednesday night, and you can hear more about Jesus there. Here's where it's at." Moriah smiled, handing one of Valery's friends a booklet from last Sunday's sermon. "You and the girls can come and hang out. We worship, then my youth pastor talks about Jesus, and then we play games till we want to go. And I made you guys some cookies," she said, pulling out a tin from her backpack and opening it, showing them the cookies she had made. "They're chocolate, and I made sure there were no nuts, in case you're allergic."

Valery didn't say a word. She looked at Moriah with a blank expression for a few moments. Then, Valery busted out in loud laughter, snatched the booklet from her friend, threw the booklet on the soccer field, got up, and stepped on it. "Come on, guys, this place is lame," Valery said, leading her gang away from the bleachers. As she passed Moriah, she brought up her hand and purposely knocked Moriah's cookies out of her hands and onto the floor. "Oops. Guess you'll have to make some more, nerd!" She laughed as she and her gang walked away. There Moriah stood, alone at the bleachers again, only this time she had to pick up broken cookie pieces from the ground.

"Well, that didn't work. She's not nicer," Moriah thought, "but I didn't do it for her to be nicer. I did it because Jesus told me to, and

He's proud of me." Moriah smiled. "At least I still have some cookies left in Mom's tin," Moriah said, taking out a clean cookie from the tin and taking a bite.

CHAPTER 4

THE VISITOR

What Moriah didn't know was that her sharing the gospel with Valery's gang didn't fall on completely deaf ears. When Moriah went to youth group that Wednesday night, she didn't expect anyone from Valery's gang to come. As she filed with the other junior high schoolers into the room set apart for them in building one, Moriah took one last glance at the church's parking lot. There, dressed in a black T-shirt and ripped blue jeans and with black hair and tons of makeup on was one of Valery's friends. Moriah couldn't believe her eyes. She walked up to the girl, her eyes and mouth open wide. They both stared at each other awkwardly for a moment; then the girl in black spoke up shyly. "Isn't this the place?"

"Yes, it is!" Moriah said, laughing out of surprise. "I'm glad you came! My name is Moriah—"

"I know," the girl said with a smile. "I liked how you talked so kindly and bravely to Valery. Nobody talks to her like that! You even offered her cookies, even though she made fun of you. That's why I came—"

"Well, come on!" Moriah interrupted. Excitedly, she grabbed the girl's hand and ran with her into the youth group. The youth group room was a large room that was unofficially split into two sides, the back and the front. Inside, up in the front of the room, facing the chairs, it had an old couch, a short coffee table, a lamp, a bookshelf filled with Bibles and teen devotionals, and a shelf with a soundboard and speakers on the walls. On the wall behind the couch, there was John 3:16 painted in graffiti lettering to look hip and cool. Inside, plastic folding chairs, bean bags, and extra chairs from the children's ministry were placed randomly around the back of the room, facing the front. Moriah and the girl quietly found a seat in the back of the room, and Moriah left her purse on her chair and went up to the front. At the front of the room, where the couch sat, the youth pastor stood up holding a microphone connected to the soundboard. The youth pastor's name was Pastor Andrew, though the teens all called him Pastor Andy. He was an adult in his early twenties with long blond hair and a short blond beard. He was tall and skinny, and all the teens loved him. He was cool, fun, and crazy all at the same time.

"Come rock it out, Mor!" he called to Moriah as she walked up to the front. Moriah was the worship leader of the youth group because she was the only one brave enough to go to the front and sing every Wednesday night. After the youth pastor handed Moriah the mic, he went out of a side door that connected the youth group to the other rooms in building one and came back with an old two-hundred-pound television set from the fifties. He twisted a few knobs and pressed some buttons, and some worship lyrics appeared on the faded curved glass screen. Moriah started to sing, and all the other junior high schoolers joined in, even Valery's friend in the back.

After two songs, Moriah sat back down with Valery's friend, and the youth pastor told the story of the prodigal son. He taught the teens about God's grace and why the story of the prodigal son is important. Afterward, the girl in black tried to hold back tears from her eyes, but it was no use. The tears began to flow. Moriah noticed she was making soft sniffling noises next to her. So Moriah got out a tissue from her purse and put her arm around the girl and tried to console her. When all the other teens went outside to play basketball like they did every Wednesday, the youth pastor went up to the girls huddled together in the back. When he came over, Moriah excused herself in order to give them some alone time. She waited outside the youth group room for quite a while, wondering why the girl was crying. All of a sudden, the girl came out, her mascara running and her eyeliner smeared, smiling. "Can I show you something?" she asked Moriah.

"Sure," Moriah said, turning to face her and holding out her hand.

"No, somewhere private."

"Oh? Come on, let's go to the ladies room," Moriah said, pulling the girl over to the restroom. They both went inside, and the girl grabbed some tissue paper, wetted it at the sink, and began patting her eyes, attempting to remove her makeup.

"Do you have some makeup remover?" the girl asked, massaging her eyes.

"Yeah, I think I do?" Moriah said, digging in her purse. She found a small tube of makeup remover and handed it to the girl. "I never got your name?" Moriah asked.

"My name's Abigail, but you can call me Abby," the girl said. "And here's what I wanted to show you. I've never shown anyone this before, so don't laugh," the girl said gravely. Then she put both of her hands on top of her head, grasped her black hair in a tight grip, and lifted her hair off of her head, revealing a bald cap underneath. Then she removed the bald cap and revealed a full head of flowing long blond hair.

"A wig!" Moriah gasped. "You wear a wig?"

"My parents wouldn't let me dye my hair, and Valery thinks any color other than black isn't cool. What was I supposed to do?" Abigail said, embarrassed. "I'm not friends with Valery anymore. She's not a real friend. Maybe we could be friends?"

"Really? That would be nice." Moriah smiled. "Come on, let's go play some basketball; it's kind of a tradition around here. Are you feeling better now?"

"Totally," Abigail smiled. Then, she threw her wig and bald cap in the trash, and they both walked over to the basketball courts.

What Abigail said was right. Valery wasn't a real friend to her. In fact, Valery wasn't a real friend to any of the girls in her clique. No one really knew for sure when the clique started, but everyone in the school knew it existed. Many teens outside the clique wanted so badly to be in it. It looked like fun, with all the girls always talking and laughing with each other, but things aren't always what they seem. In reality, the girls in the clique were only in the clique because they cared so much about what others thought of them. They wanted to be liked, they wanted to be popular, and they wanted to be in the in crowd. So they put up with Valery and all the strict rules and regulations to be in the clique.

Valery was the leader because she was the most popular and the most controlling. She was a natural born leader, and she used her gifts for her own gain. She secretly wished to be the most liked and the most popular girl in school, and her clique made her feel that way. Not to mention all the help she got from them on a day-to-day basis. Valery was also a great negotiator; she could get anyone to do her bidding. This especially included her six friends. She always bossed them around worse than anyone. At lunchtime, the clique normally sat in the middle of the cafeteria, and after Abigail brought Valery her lunch, like she did every lunchtime, Valery would demand her daily updates from the group. "Gretchen! What's the news?" Valery would shout.

"Well, you know how Molly said she hated Ava? Well, Molly totally stole Ava's boyfriend, and I heard Ava still doesn't know!" Gretchen whispered in Valery's ear. Gretchen was Valery's main gossip. All the girls in Valery's clique had to wear some form of black clothing, but each girl dressed a little differently. Gretchen always wore pretty dresses with a black jacket and her hair down and in the front in order to hide her phone when she took photos of good gossip scenes. "See, here's Ava and the guy. I don't know much about him yet," Gretchen whispered, showing Valery her phone.

"Azul! Cute boy alert!" Valery said, taking Gretchen's phone and passing it to a girl named Azul further down the table. Azul always wore black dresses with tons of sparkly, expensive jewelry and ornaments. She wore her hair down and behind her ears, loving to show off her intricate, dangly earrings. She was Valery's boy expert; she knew every boy in school.

"That's Tim; he's new. He's kind of cute, but he picks his nose. Stay clear," Azul warned, giving Gretchen back her phone, and all the girls said, "Ew!" in unison.

"Bertha! Status report!" Valery yelled. Bertha was Valery's tech giant. She knew everything there was to know about social media and the internet. Bertha always wore a black T-shirt with different-colored extremely short skirts. She always wore all of her hair on one side to hide her phone from the teachers during class.

"Your selfie with Hildey during your morning workout is totally trending! And what you said about how all boys are cute is getting repeated like a million times!" Bertha said, continuously texting on her phone without looking up. Hildey, her real name was Brunhilda, was also one of Valery's main six. She kept Valery in shape and offered Valery a little protection since she was super tough. She always wore her hair in a side ponytail, and she always wore tight black turtleneck sweaters like Valery, but she hated skirts, so she put on jeans.

"Dorcas, what are we going to do in history?" Valery asked, taking a bite of her salad. Dorcas was Valery's ace in the hole when it came to schoolwork. Dorcas was super smart, and in order to remind Valery of this, she began wearing fake glasses, putting her hair in a bun, and putting a pencil on her ear because she thought it made her look smart.

"We are going to have a test on the thirteen colonies. I'll help you study before lunch is over," Dorcus said, sipping her apple juice. Dorcus always had to help Valery study or figure out math problems at lunch. Last of all was Abigail, who Valery always called Gail even though she hated to be called Gail. She got into the group because she wore ripped and frayed jeans before they were popular. That's because her family was too poor to buy her new jeans when her old ones got worn out. She always did all of the grunt work of the group, carrying Valery's books, combing Valery's hair, and agreeing with everything Valery said and did.

On a typical, average day, Abigail would spend the entire school day doing whatever Valery was doing, and then she would say goodbye to the gang and begin her after-school tasks. After school, Abigail had to walk over, pick up her twin brother and sister from their elementary school, and walk them home. The only problem was that her little brother and sister often had after-school clubs and events that her parents signed them up for. So, every day after school, Abigail would have to wait an hour or more until it was time to walk over, pick them up, and walk them back home. In order to not completely waste her time, Abigail normally went over to the track and field track at her school, put on her running shoes, and ran for miles for fun. She loved running and exercise. She loved how good her body felt after a good run.

After that, she would usually finish her homework until it was time to head over to the elementary school. When it was time to pick up her siblings from their school, Abigail wasn't always in the best of moods. "Come on, I don't got all day!" she would shout at them as they came running out.

"Sorry," her little brother, Bobby, would respond sadly.

"How was your day?" her little sister, Lily, would ask in a shy voice.

"Fine," Abigail would say in an angry tone, and they would walk the rest of the way home in silence. Abigail wasn't really angry at her siblings. The truth was she was angry at a lot of things. Her family was very poor. Their father had to work two and a half jobs just to barely pay the rent and keep a roof over their heads, while their mother had to work night shifts at her job in order to make scarcely enough to put some food on the table. When Abigail and her siblings would come home, which was a rented house that they shared with another family, they would have to quietly sneak past the other family's half of the house in order to get to their two separate rooms. Abigail finally had her own room in this rented house. She had to share a room with her siblings in the many other rented spaces they had previously lived in, but having her own room didn't keep out all her troubles. Her parents often fought and threatened to divorce each other on a daily basis. She would often hear these fights, being in the next room closest to her parents, and she would put in her headphones connected to her grandmother's old radio and try to drown out the yelling, but that never worked. This was how Abigail's life normally went, that is until the day Moriah went up to Valery at the bleachers.

On that day, every girl in the clique was shocked that Moriah had the courage to talk so kindly back to Valery and share what she believed. "Doesn't she know who she's talking to? Valery could ruin her rep," Abigail thought as Moriah began telling them about the Bible. As Moriah talked, Abigail listened. She had to pretend she wasn't listening by twisting her face into an angry expression and once in a while staring at Valery and giving Valery a smirk to make sure Valery knew she was on her side. Abigail could see that Valery was very angry and getting angrier with every word Moriah spoke. As it so happened, Moriah handed Abigail the booklet with her church's address on it. "I like this girl. She's not afraid of being laughed at or being made unpopular by Valery. I want that," Abby thought. Suddenly, Abigail noticed that Moriah had stopped talking and was reaching around to grab her backpack off of her shoulders. Abigail knew Valery enough to know that soon Valery was going to let her have it. Quickly, Abigail snuck her old flip phone, which used to be her grandma's as well, out of her jean pocket.

As Moriah showed the girls her cookies and distracted them, Abigail snapped a photo of the address on the front of the booklet and quickly tucked her phone back in her pocket. Then, just as Abigail had guessed, Valery turned to her and grabbed the booklet from her hand and threw it on the ground. "Here it comes." Abigail winced, expecting Valery to blow up on Moriah, but she didn't. Instead, she just stepped on the booklet and ordered all of them to follow her. Abigail thought this very strange. Even when Valery knocked the cookies out of Moriah's hands, Abigail was expecting more.

When they left Moriah, they all weren't sure where they were headed. The reason they had gone in search of a new place to eat lunch was that the cafeteria was off limits to students for a few weeks because of water damage. After walking a few yards away, and once everyone was sure they were out of earshot of Moriah, Dorcus spoke up. "Val, where are we going?"

"Quiet!" Valery shouted, and Dorcus hid behind Brunhilda. Abigail thought about Moriah and her courage. She thought about how Moriah was able to eat lunch alone and how she herself hated to be alone. "Gail! I'm warm!" Valery shouted at Abigail. That meant that Abigail was to give Valery her water bottle, but Abigail was so lost in thought she really didn't hear Valery. "Gail! I'm waiting! Gail!"

"Oh, sorry!" Abigail said, reaching into her old pink backpack that she had since she was little and taking out Valery's water bottle. Valery made Abigail carry around her water bottle just so that she didn't have to. As Abigail handed Valery her water bottle, Valery's eyes narrowed and she stared intently at Abigail. "Hey, Gail, why don't you go over and see if there's a nice spot for us over by the drinking fountain," Valery said in a sweet tone. Abigail knew that voice all too well. She had watched Valery use it whenever she wanted to trick the teachers or convince an unsuspecting victim to tell her all she wanted to know. Abigail had a funny feeling form in her heart, and she knew something wasn't right. So like always, she simply did as she was told. She went over to the drinking fountain a few yards away, but then she remembered Valery hadn't given her back the water bottle for her to hold, and she turned around and walked back over to the group to retrieve the water bottle. All of a sudden, she saw they were all huddled in a group. They were all whispering, and this is what she heard. "Gretchen! I want you to find out more about our little yes girl. See if she's been talking to anyone I don't like," Valery said angrily.

"She has been acting a little funny," Dorcus said, trying to get back in Valery's good graces. "She never talks! She's always just following us around, and that wig! Who is she kidding! Right guys!" All the girls laughed.

Then Azul spoke up. "I think she's single 'cause of her weird family."

"Yeah, and have you seen the way she runs! It's pathetic!" Brunhilda added, and all the girls laughed again.

"Bertha! How about you look around online. See if you can find out what makes her tick. Now quiet! She'll be back soon," Valery said, looking around for Abigail. Abigail couldn't believe her ears. She thought that Valery and the others liked her, that Valery and the others were her friends. They had known each other for a few years now, going to each other's houses, talking about boys, and going to parties. Abigail wanted to cry, but she knew the girls would get suspicious if she waited too long where she was. So she walked closer to the group; then Valery noticed her. Valery waved her hands, bidding Abigail to come over. Abigail walked over with her head held high. "Gail! Did you find anything? Your eyes are the best for finding stuff," Valery said sweetly, putting her arm around Abigail's shoulders.

"No, not really," Abigail responded in a sad tone.

"What's wrong Gail? You're always so cheerful! Look at that hair, isn't it beautiful girls?" Valery said, touching Abigail's wig.

The girls all nodded their heads yes, and Dorcus said in a happy tone, "It's so natural!"

Anger filled up in Abigail's heart. "What do they think? I'm an idiot!" Abigail thought. She wanted to cry. She wanted to yell. "I came to your birthday party! That's how you treat me! You talk behind my back!" she thought as she looked at Dorcus, giving her a thumbs up. In that moment it was too much to take. "I gotta go," Abigail said, and she ran away.

All throughout the day, Bertha texted her. "Where are you? Where'd you go? You okay? Valery is mad." After school, Abigail didn't go to the track and field track for fear of Brunhilda being there. She instead went over to her sibling's school right away and waited on the front steps of the elementary school for them. Sadly, she looked through her phones texts. She read all the jokes she shared with Azul, all the images she sent to Brunhilda, and all the messages she sent to Valery. Abigail always knew that a girl's membership in the clique was always threatened. If a better follower came along, Valery would normally kick one girl out of the group and ask the other girls to shun her. Abigail just never thought it would be her.

"Why was I even friends with them?" she thought as she sat alone. "I guess 'cause I just wanted to be liked." She thought about this for a moment. She decided she would delete all of the selfies that Valery put on her phone. As she opened her photos on her flip phone, she saw the address of the church. "That's right. That girl Moriah invited us. I bet Val wouldn't be caught dead there. So that's where I'll go!" Abigail said out loud, and she did just that. On Wednesday, she headed over to the church from her home; as it turned out, the church was only two blocks away. When she was there, the youth pastor's sermon really hit home. Abigail's parents had taken her to church during Easter and Christmas a few times when she was younger, but Abby never really cared about it before that night. That evening, when Youth Pastor Andrew talked about the father and the prodigal son and explained the parable, Abigail wanted so badly for her life to be like the prodigal son's. She wanted to be loved as much as the prodigal son.

When the youth pastor spoke about the grace that only Jesus gives, Abigail wanted Jesus to be her Savior. That's when the tears came, and that's when Moriah left Youth Pastor Andrew and Abigail alone. After they talked together for a little bit and she got answers to some of her questions, Abigail prayed to the Lord for her salvation, and she was saved. It was then that she knew she didn't want to be fake anymore. She didn't want to pretend her life was perfect just because she was afraid of what others thought of her. She didn't want to wear a wig she didn't need just because some people didn't like her hair. That's why she wanted to show Moriah her real hair; she wanted to be real.

That night, as Abby and Moriah headed over to the basketball courts, the other teens had already started playing. "Hi, guys! Do you have room for two more?" Moriah called to them.

"What? Miss 'always the ref' is gonna play?" one of the boys laughed. Moriah normally never played basketball with the others. She hated sports and preferred to keep score or be the referee. However, tonight she thought it would be best for her new friend to play some ball in order for her to get her mind on something fun, and she knew she had to join in to make sure Abby was comfortable.

"Ha ha. Very funny. Come on, let's do girls versus boys. Five against six," Moriah offered.

"But there are six boys; that's not fair!" one of the girls complained.

"We can beat them! It will be easy!" Moriah taunted.

"Wanna bet! You're on!" the boys laughed. The game was on, and Abigail was very nervous. She had never played any sport before, since Valery hated all things athletic.

She at first tried just to stay out of the way, but that didn't work very long. Soon Moriah got hold of the ball and passed it to her, shouting, "Go, Abby! Shoot it!" Abby looked and saw a whole group of boys charging at her. She screamed and threw the ball into the bushes near-by. It wasn't her finest moment, and the boys all laughed. "It's okay. You will do better next time," Moriah said, putting her hand on Abigail's shoulder. That was true; Abigail did do better the next time. Moriah passed her the ball again, and Abby tried to make it in the basket, but she missed. "Good shot!" Moriah shouted to her. Abigail felt very pleased. She really enjoyed running around, dodging, and passing. She loved the excitement, the laughing, and the adrenaline she felt trying to make a basket. Finally, it was getting late, and the score was boys eight and girls seven. One of the taller girls made a basket, and the game was tied.

"How 'bout we stop here and call it a night," one of the boys said, trying to catch his breath.

"What's wrong? Scared of a little competition from the new girl?" Abigail taunted. Everyone looked shocked, and Moriah laughed. She was glad that Abby felt comfortable enough to joke around.

The boys all gave impressed smiles; then one of them picked up the ball and said, "Let's go! For the win." The ball was tossed in the air. Abigail jumped for it and missed. It went to the boy's side; one of them began dribbling the ball. He passed it to another boy, who passed it to another boy. One of the girls blocked the pass and got hold of the ball. She looked and saw Abigail over by the net.

"Abby! Go for it!" she yelled, passing Abigail the ball. With a huge grin, Abby made the shot. The ball went up, balanced on the rim, sat there for a moment, and leaned left and right; the tension was intense. It went in, and Abby had scored.

All the girls cheered, and the boys all patted her on the back and said, "Good game! That was awesome! You got skills, girl!" That was the night that Abby learned she loved sports and from then on, she was always the first one on the basketball court after youth group and after church on Sundays.

CHAPTER 5

THE OFFSIDE

The next day, Abby came to school dressed differently than normal. She hated putting so much makeup on in the morning. She didn't like the way most makeup looked on her eyes. It dried her skin, and she hated the way it felt. She also hated sweating on her forehead and having to worry about her mascara running. So for the first time, she came to school without any makeup on, and for the first time, she didn't wear her wig but let her blond hair down. Also for the first time, she wore an outfit without any black in it. She wore a yellow dress that her aunt had bought her for her birthday, along with some pink sandals. When Valery and the clique saw her, their eyes practically came out of their heads. They wouldn't speak a word to her, but Abby didn't mind. She didn't care what they thought of her anymore. The only one who's opinion of her mattered to her was Jesus. Knowing that Jesus wanted her to be forgiving, Abby went up to them and said very sweetly, "I heard what you said about me. I forgive you, and I think it would be best if we went our separate ways. I hope you all take what Moriah said seriously 'cause it's the truth." After that, Abigail tried hard to forgive them each time the pain of what happened came up in her heart again, and that would take some time. Some wounds take longer to heal from than others, especially betrayal. In the meantime, she hung out with Moriah, texting and eating lunch together at the bleachers.

That following Monday, as Moriah was sitting in her last class of the day, she realized she had left her special book at the soccer field bleachers. So as soon as the dismissal bell rang, she charged to the bleachers and was surprised to see Abigail already there, sitting watching the soccer team practice. "Hey, you left your book," she said, handing Moriah the book.

"Thank you," Moriah said, taking a seat next to her friend. "Why are you here?"

"Ya know, when I was friends with Val, we sometimes used to come over here and make fun of the soccer team. We said some really mean stuff," Abby said, feeling ashamed.

"Why?"

"You know Valery. She makes fun of anything she doesn't understand or can't do herself. 'Cause we were so rude, the coach banished us from the bleachers and the games."

"Why has he not asked you to leave then?"

Abby shrugged. "I bet he doesn't recognize me with blond hair and no makeup on." The girls sat in silence for a moment.

Then, Moriah said in a consoling tone, "Well, you are a different person now, and you still haven't yet told me why you're sitting here."

"I wish I could be out there!" Abigail said in a yearning voice. "Look at them! It looks so awesome! Too bad tryouts were during the summer. I would love to play." Moriah turned and stared at the soccer field with Abigail. All around, girls, dressed in blue and white jerseys with white numbers on the back, black athletic shorts, knee-high socks with shin pads, and cleats, were running to and fro. In the center of the action was the coach, blowing his whistle and giving instruction. He also wore a blue and white jersey and shorts, but his jersey had written on the back of it his title "Coach" in big white letters. He was kind and authoritative all at the same time. He was an African American man who always wore his glasses on his face and his silver whistle around his neck. His phone began to ring, so he blew his whistle and called for a break.

The coach walked over to the bleachers and stopped a few yards in front of Moriah and Abby and answered his phone. "Oh no! Really? Can't she just skip a few practices to bring up her grades? That bad, huh? All right. I understand. You too. Goodbye."

"What's up, coach?" a girl with a white number eighteen on the back of her jersey ran up and asked.

"That was Alisha's mom. That makes our fourth drop out this month, and she was our best striker."

"That means we won't have enough players for our next match, coach!" another girl with a number nine came up and yelled in an anxious tone.

"I know, it looks like I'll have to reopen tryouts, see if any of the girls I turned down will come back. They may not; most of them went and joined the town league. Ugh, and that means I'm going to have to make time on the school schedule for another tryout date! Mrs. Snider's gonna be furious!" the coach said, putting his hand to his head and shaking his head miserably.

"Hurry!" Moriah said, grabbing Abby by the hand and pulling her off the bleaches and toward the coach.

"What're we doing?" Abby gasped with a shocked expression.

"Coach!" Moriah yelled, standing up straight and speaking in her most professional tone. "I believe it would be an absolute shame if you did not allow my friend to try out for your team immediately! She's ready, she's willing, she has an hour after school free every day, and it is her dream to join your team!"

"I didn't see you at tryouts?" the coach said, looking at Abigail.

"It is a very new dream, sir," Moriah said with a smile. "And she's already here, and we know about your sad dilemma. If you let her join, you wouldn't have to set up another tryout date, and then you won't have to bother Mrs. Snider." The coach thought about this for a moment, rubbing his chin.

Then with a grin and a chuckle he said, "All right, no one joins my team without trying out. It's only fair that you try out like everybody else. Tell you what, our next game is in two weeks. You come this Friday and show me what you got. If you impress me, I'll let you join. At least that way we'll have enough players for our next match."

"Thank you so very much, sir! You won't be disappointed! You'll see!" Moriah said, pulling Abby away from the coach.

"Hold on there, what's your name?" the coach asked.

"My name's Abigail sir," Abby said, shaking his hand timidly.

"Gail!" a girl yelled behind them. Moriah and Abby turned to see the whole team staring at them, and one player with the number forty on her jersey walking up to them with an angry expression. She shouted, "You're Gail! Valery's friend! She's one of the girls you said couldn't come back, coach!" The team's blank expressions changed to stares of anger and disgust. The coach looked at Abigail with a puzzled face.

"Is this true?" he asked her.

"Yes, and well, I'm sorry for what I did. If I hurt any of your feelings in the past," Abigail said to the team; then she turned to the coach and said, "I'm not that person anymore, and I'm not friends with Valery anymore. I know what I did was wrong, and I'm really, really, really sorry! I really want to join the team, sir."

"Well that's good enough for me. Come on Friday," the coach said; then he took out his phone, dialed a number, and began a call. He walked away, and once he was far enough away, the team suddenly encircled Moriah and Abby before they could walk away.

With angry expressions, arms crossed, and scowls from every direction, the girl with the number forty came into the center and confronted Abby. "What is this? Some kind of joke? Did you really think you could just walk onto the field and join?"

"Isn't that what you did?" Moriah said in an annoyed tone; her face was cross and an anger formed in her heart for the defense of her friend.

"Shut it, this is between us and her!" one of the players yelled at Moriah.

"If you threaten my friend, you threaten me!" she yelled back.

"We haven't threatened anyone yet," the leader of the girls said in a suggestive tone that made a shiver go up Abigail's back. "You hypocrite! First you mock us and our team. Now you want to join!" the leader yelled; then leaning into Abigail's face, she whispered, "Come on Friday, and we'll make you really sorry."

The coach came back and blew his whistle. "All right ladies! Back to work! Set up the cones!" The team dispersed, and Moriah grabbed Abby's hand and ran far away from the field, but she didn't stop there. She kept running until they made it to the library's front entrance.

"Moriah! I don't know anything about soccer!" Abby yelled when they stopped running.

"I know," Moriah said, opening the library door and holding it open for Abby.

"I've never played before! Why did we do that! I gotta get ready! Why are we at the library?"

"If I am going to help you, I have to learn a few things about the game myself. We have five days and no time to lose," Moriah said, gesturing for Abby to enter the library.

She did; then she turned to face Moriah and asked, "You're gonna help me?"

"Of course! What are friends for? Besides it was me who got you into this in the first place." Moriah laughed. She got to work grabbing book after book off the shelfs and handing them to Abby to hold. All of them about soccer strategies, training, skills, pro athletes, nutrition, stretches, and much more.

The next day at lunch, Moriah started Abby's training. "This book says you should eat healthy and not have junk food," Moriah said, reading in one of the books.

"So none of your cookies?" Abby chuckled.

"Nope." Moriah laughed, then she continued reading. "It says you need to drink plenty of water, to stay hydrated."

"I already drink three bottles of water a day," Abby said, removing her little water bottle from her backpack and taking a sip.

"Well, let's shoot for four today, and make sure to eat all your apple slices," Moriah said, staring at Abby's lunch tray she had picked up at the school's lunch line.

Later, after school they met at the concrete basketball courts next to the soccer field for Abby's training. Abby put on her PE uniform, which was a gray T-shirt and mesh shorts with the school's logo on them. She also started wearing her running shoes and her hair in a ponytail more often. Before they started stretching and training, both of the girls prayed and lifted up their request to God. Abigail wanted to glorify the Lord with her playing. Moriah wanted to help Abby the best she could, even though she didn't even like sports. After they finished praying, Moriah coached Abigail from the library books about stretching and warming up. Abby worked hard and stretched more muscles than she knew she had.

"I'm starting to doubt these books know what they're talking about," she said wearily.

"This one was written by a pro midfielder."

"Well, I'd like to see him try and become a pro in five days!" Abby complained.

"Don't worry. Come on, we have forty more minutes till you have to pick up the twins. Let's do some more stretches and footwork," Moriah said, looking through another book. Abigail spent twenty more minutes training hard. Then Moriah took out a tennis ball from her bag. "Some pros practice with a tennis ball."

"What?"

"Yeah, they pretend it's a soccer ball, then maneuvering the soccer ball won't seem as hard."

"How about practicing with a soccer ball so maneuvering a soccer ball isn't so hard!" Abigail shouted.

"You can do it! Let's try," Moriah said, putting the tennis ball down. Moriah read Abby paragraph after paragraph of the best way to control the ball. Abby struggled, but she didn't give up. Before she knew it, it was time for her to cool down. She did her cool-down routine and changed into her regular jeans and pink blouse.

When she came out of the girl's locker room, she fixed her ponytail and sighed. "How am I supposed to get better if we don't practice with the ball for longer than ten minutes?"

"We will get faster."

"But we only have five days!"

"You can do this; pray and I'll pray too. Here, practice with this whenever you have time, and when you get home make sure to drink some more water," Moriah said, giving Abby the tennis ball. Abby did. On her way home, while walking with the twins, she practiced the maneuvers Moriah showed her in the books, and she drank a lot more water. At home, once she was done with her homework, she practiced controlling the tennis ball and dribbling it between her feet. She worked very hard, and she made sure to go to bed early to get plenty of rest. The next day, she had much better control of the tennis ball, and her dribbling improved as well.

Moriah began texting her photos and videos of famous players doing spins and turns and step overs. Abigail studied their techniques and practiced them with her little brother's soccer ball right before she went to bed. Three days before Friday, she was able to drink four bottles of water a day. However, even with all of her physical preparation, she still didn't feel really ready. Something inside of her didn't feel right. So on Wednesday at youth group, she waited after the other teens left to talk to Pastor Andrew.

"Are you coming, Abby? I convinced the others to play soccer instead of basketball tonight. It will give you some more experience with the game," Moriah said to her after the sermon.

"Yeah, I'll be there in a sec," she said in a sad tone. Moriah had a feeling Abby wanted to be alone with Pastor Andrew. So she put her hand on Abby's shoulder, nodded, and waited outside for her.

"What's wrong, Abby? Is it that soccer tryout you and Moriah told me about?" Youth Pastor Andrew asked, taking a seat next to her.

"What if the girls on the soccer team are right? What if I am a hypocrite? I said some really nasty things to them before I knew better."

"Personally, I don't think you're acting like a hypocrite. I think what you're really asking is can a person be someone different after they accept Christ? Absolutely! When we accept Christ, we receive His Holy Spirit, and we live our lives to glorify and please the Lord. I mean, think about Galatians 2:20, which says, 'I have been crucified with Christ and I no longer live, but Christ lives in me. The life I now live in the body, I live by faith in the Son of God, who loved me and gave himself for me.' Or how about 2 Corinthians 2:17, which says, 'Therefore, if anyone is in Christ, the new creation has come: The old has gone, the new is here!' Christ lives in you now, and you're living your life for Him." Pastor Andrew could see Abigail wasn't satisfied with his answer. So he asked, "But how do you feel about the situation? Do you feel like a hypocrite?"

Abby paused and stared down at the floor. She remembered the words that those girls yelled at her. Her heart became gloomy, and she nodded her head yes sadly in response.

"Well, whether you are or not, God's grace is sufficient for every part of us, even the hypocritical parts. You know, some people believe all Christians are hypocrites, and this is a very wrong assumption. What they don't understand is that you should not base the deeds of some as pertaining to the entire group. Not every Christian is a hypocrite. As for your situation, you prayed to God and asked for His forgiveness; I remember 'cause I was there. Now about you making fun of those girls in the past. You apologized, and you're never gonna do it again, right?" Abby nodded her head no passionately. "You are sincerely sorry for what you did, and you honestly regret what you did. You repented of your actions, and you attempted to make amends. You can't take your words back, but you can apologize for them. Does that summarize things pretty well?"

"It sure does." Abby smiled.

"Then in my humble opinion, you're not being a hypocrite. Go to those tryouts and continue to pray. God loves you and those girls, remember that." After their talk, Abby felt better and more confident. After hard training all week, Friday finally came. During lunch at the bleachers, Moriah and Abby ate quietly, which was unusual for them.

"I know you are nervous." Moriah coughed, breaking the silence. "I have something for you. My mom and I picked it out from the sports store," she said, taking a neatly wrapped box from her backpack.

"Thanks!" Abby gasped, opening it excitedly. Once it was open, she lifted out of it a pink and white jersey with a white number seven on the back. "It's beautiful!" she said, with a tear forming in her eye. She didn't want to ask her parents for athletic clothes. She felt they were struggling with money enough already.

"And we bought you some pink shin pads and socks, like the white ones the other girls were wearing." Abigail picked these things out of the box as if they were fragile diamonds. "And I am sure the coach will loan you some cleats. You are going to do great! I know you will!" Moriah and Abby hugged and prayed one more time before Abby's tryout.

After school, Abby marched onto the soccer field, wearing her pink jersey, black athletic shorts, and pink shin pads and socks. The coach did allow her to borrow a pair of cleats, and they, thankfully, fit like a glove. With a look of determination, Abby took a pink puffy hair tie out of her backpack and tied her hair in a high ponytail. "You ready?" the coach said, holding his clipboard. Abby gave one last look over to Moriah, who was sitting on the bleachers, holding up a sign she had made with Abby's name on it.

Abby waved to her; then she turned to the coach and responded, "I'm ready." The coach walked her over to the other girls on the field. They all gave Abigail foul looks, and the girl with the number forty sneered.

"All right, ladies, Abby here wants to try out today. Sabrinna, how about you go over and prepare for a short pass from Abby." One of the girls went over and stood to the side of Abby a few steps away. Abby took a deep breath and did a short pass the best she could. The pass was fine. "Nice job, kid," the coach commented, writing quickly on his clipboard. "Let's try for a long driven pass." Sabrinna turned around, ran forward, and stood to the right, far away from Abby. Abby held her breath, prepared her shot, and made a satisfactory long pass. "Fine," the coach said when he saw where her pass landed. They spent the rest of the time going through the works of an average tryout. After a long while, the tryout was almost over, but then the coach decided to do something out of the ordinary. Maybe he saw some special talent in Abby. Whatever the reason, he suddenly blew his whistle to get his team's attention. "Now let's try some defensive work. Karen, line up," the coach commanded, and the girl wearing the number forty went over and lined up instinctually a few yards in front of the goal mouth. "Katy, position!" the coach yelled, placing a soccer ball in front of Abby. Another girl, in a slightly different patterned jersey and gloves, went and crouched inside the goal. Then he said in a relaxed manner. "I want you to try and get the ball past one of my center backs. Maybe try to make a goal, if you want to."

The girl wearing the number forty was defending the goal ahead of the goalie and close enough to Abigail to be heard. When the coach stepped to the sideline, she grinned and whispered, "I'm gonna enjoy this, hypocrite." Abigail grinned back. She remembered what Pastor Andy had told her, and she knew, whatever happened, that she was loved by the Lord. Quickly, she bowed her head and prayed silently. The coach blew the whistle; the game was on.

The girl with the number forty charged forward. Abby spun all the way around, moving her and the ball to the right. She kicked and dribbled it forward at an amazing speed. As Abigail ran past her, the girl with the number forty turned around and was so shocked that she stood still. With her jaw dropped, she quickly stopped wondering how Abigail had gotten past her and ran toward Abby. This all happened in a matter of seconds, but it felt like it was happening in slow motion to Abby and the other girls. Noticing the girl with the number forty closing in fast on her left side, Abby slowed down and stopped the ball, causing the girl with the number forty to slow down with her. Before she caught up to the ball, Abigail powerfully kicked the ball past her to the left and bolted past her. The girl with the number forty was shocked, but she didn't stop. She tried to closely follow Abigail and intercept the ball. Abigail expected this and successfully faked maneuvering the ball one way while stepping over the ball and truthfully going the opposite way. She successfully tricked the girl with the number forty to go the opposite way than where she was heading. In this way, Abigail freed up space for herself. She was faster than any of the girls on the team had expected, and they all were stunned. Suddenly, it was just her and the goalie. Abby went for a shot, but then she saw out of the corner of her eye the girl with the number forty on her jersey begin a sliding tackle. Desperately, sliding on the floor on her side, sticking out her foot, meaning to kick the ball out of the way of Abby's feet, the girl with the number forty on her jersey was coming in fast.

There was no time to lose. Abby kicked and jumped at the same time, successfully jumping over the girl with the number forty on her jersey. The ball soared through the air. The goalie was surprised and looked up at it in dismay. She jumped for it. It sailed right through her grip and hit the net. Abby had scored.

The coach blew the whistle. He walked over to them with a huge grin. "I think I just found my new player!" he said, putting both his hands on Abigail's shoulders. "You're still very rough, but I believe in another week, we'll begin to smooth out some of those rough edges." Suddenly, three boys ran out of nowhere onto the field and began kicking some of the soccer balls on the other side of the field. The coach saw them and started walking toward them shouting, "Hey! You boys stop that!"

He walked away, leaving the girls together on the field. The girl with the number forty on her shirt got up off the ground, brushed off her jersey, and walked over to Abby. "You're good. Better than any of us thought. My name's Karen. Look, as I did most of the talking already, I think I can speak for the team when I say we forgive you for what you said, now that we're on the same team and all." The rest of the team all nodded and agreed.

"Thanks." Abby smiled.

Karen nodded her head and added quietly, "I hope you won't hold anything I said against me. I'm sorry."

"Sure. I forgive you too. It's totally cool," Abby said, giving her a fist bump. Moriah came running onto the field and hugged Abby.

"That was awesome!" she yelled. She was really excited for a girl who hated sports. From then on, Abby was the Lancer Girls Soccer Team's top player. She trained hard, and after a while, she became the Lancer Girls Soccer Team's new striker. She also played on the school's girl basketball team and track team.

It was weeks later when Moriah told Abigail about a strange, poor boy at church who had stolen the pastor's Bible and returned it. Then, when Moriah saw the boy at school, she could hardly believe it; she only had time to grab Abby and pull her over to him.

CHAPTER 6

EVERYDAY DAY

That's how all three of them, David, Moriah, and Abigail, found themselves walking down the hallway together on that mid-October day. As they walked along, the school bell rang, telling the students to go to their classes. Abby waved goodbye to Moriah and David and silently headed in another direction toward her next class. David watched her go and forgot where he was going and walked right into a pole. Moriah was so busy reading David's schedule that she didn't notice this until it was too late. "Are you okay?" she asked, helping him to his feet and trying to hold back her laughter.

"Yeah, I'm okay," he responded, shaking his head, trying to regain his dignity.

Moriah thought it best to quickly change the subject and asked, "What is your name?"

"My name's David. Where'd you say we're going?"

"It says here your first class is music fundamentals. That is my first class too! That is so cool! You are going to love Mr. C! He's so funny! I love music! I've been playing the drums since I was six years old, and I've been singing for even longer than that." After walking a few steps, suddenly Moriah stopped in front of a very small door with five small concrete steps leading up to it. This door was much smaller than the doors surrounding it, and David almost completely missed it and walked a few steps ahead before he realized Moriah wasn't walking beside him anymore. He doubled back over to where she was standing and stared at the door with her.

She handed him back his schedule with a sigh. "Yep, this is good old room seventeen and a half."

"This is the music room?" David asked. He had never seen a music room before, but he figured that this one had to be very small in order to have such a small door.

Moriah laughed. "This is just the door we have to use to get in. There are some huge doors in the back where we bring in the instruments and stuff. It's actually really big! Come see!" The two teens climbed the five concrete steps and went inside the tiny door. Once David was inside, he saw how ginormous the room really was. On one side of the room, stretched from corner to corner, were some very long foldable metal bleachers three levels high. In front of the bleachers were many foldable plastic chairs with music stands in front of them. These chairs were neatly organized into a half circle facing two big whiteboards and a podium on the other side of the room. Inside these chairs sat students with many different types of instruments. Some had flutes, clarinets, cellos, violins, acoustic guitars, and many other instruments that David had never seen or heard before. To the left of the chairs and bleachers, closest to the small door, stood many different types of drums. Moriah took a seat at a full drum set. Then she pulled out of her pack two drumsticks with her initials engraved on them.

"Well, it looks like we have ourselves a new band member!" a loud voice echoed from across the room. On the left side of the room, farthest from the small door, stood an elegant grand piano and the two giant doors that Moriah had spoken of earlier. David looked over and saw a man rise from the grand piano and walk over to the podium. He picked up a very short shiny stick and tapped it three times on the podium. "Class, take your places. We have a new face joining us today," he announced, and instantly, all the students sat up straight in their chairs and held their instruments ready to play. "Come here, young man!" he said as he gestured to David to come closer. David was attempting to hide in the doorway and go unnoticed. Realizing he had been spotted, he timidly walked over to the podium and stuck his hand out to the teacher.

"My name's David," he said in a deeper voice than usual. He was trying to look casual and calm, when in reality all he could think about was all the other teens staring at him. This was especially hard for David, who had never been to a middle school before and hadn't been in a classroom for so long.

"Nice to meet you David. My name is Mr. C." The teacher smiled, shaking his hand. "Tell me, what do you play?"

"Play? I like video games?" David said, confused. Snickers erupted quietly from around the class.

"No, David. Play as in what's your instrument? If you picked this class you must have some interest in music?"

"I didn't pick this class. The office gave it to me."

"Mrs. Snider!" Mr. C moaned under his breath. "All right, David, what's your favorite kind of music?"

"Well, I like rap."

"Okay, do you sing at all?" David was taken aback. He had never sung in all his life and especially not now in front of all his peers. He was so conflicted, he didn't answer. "Here, let's try something basic. I'll sing a note, and you try to match me. Okay?" David stammered in response. "It'll be easy; follow after me," Mr. C said in a kind tone. He proceeded to sing a small note. There was a pause as he gestured for David to sing the same. David froze and stared at all the faces staring at him up in the front. The class all had blank expressions, some even seemed angry. Sweat began to form on David's forehead. His face became paler than usual. His hands began to fidget with his shirt collar. He held his breath. His throat became hoarse, and his eyes furiously went back and forth, scanning the room for an escape. His heartbeat was ringing in his ears like the pounding of a drum. At last, his eyes rested on Moriah at the drums, she was the only one smiling. With a grin, she encouragingly gave him a thumbs up. David took in a deep breath.

"I'm not getting out of this," he thought, giving in. "Can you repeat that?" he asked the teacher. Mr. C repeated the note. David took in a deeper breath and attempted to match the note. Surprisingly, he did quite well. Mr. C resounded another note. David matched that one as well. Mr. C sang a harder note, and David matched it perfectly.

"Stop joking! You really had me going. Who put you up to this? Was it Tommy?" Mr. C laughed.

"Sir, I don't?" David stuttered, feeling embarrassed at his singing.

"Stop messing around! Why didn't you tell me that you can sing! They just meant to put you in choir instead of band, that's all," Mr. C said, typing on his laptop that he kept in a cubby inside the podium.

"But, sir, I don't wanna be in choir," David protested. He really didn't want to be in band either, but playing an instrument sounded better than ever singing again.

"Fine, then if you're going to be in band you must play an instrument," Mr. C said, now beginning to be annoyed. David looked around.

"How about the guitar?" Moriah suggested from the drums. She was just trying to be helpful. Everyone's eyes turned to her, then back to David.

"Sure, whatever." David shrugged. He wouldn't have cared if she had suggested the sousaphone in that moment. At this point, he just wanted to get away from all the eyes staring at him.

"Fine, go over by Carlos. He'll show you where we keep our guitars," Mr. C said; then he tapped his stick on the podium and led the school's band in a melody. Carlos helped David find a guitar that fit him just right. David spent the rest of the time in band simply trying to make the guitar make a sound with his fingers on the strings. Carlos showed him what to do and taught him the right way to hold the guitar. Mr. C came over and helped him as well. David enjoyed trying to make the guitar play, and he really liked the idea of him playing the guitar one day. In fact, when he got home that day, he asked Mr. Gardien if he could have a tutor come and help him every day after school until he could play adequately. Mr. Gardien got David's parents' permission, and they agreed. They bought David the finest guitars on the market, one acoustic guitar, one electric guitar, and one acoustic and electric guitar. However, to his dismay, that wouldn't be the end of David's singing career, not by any means.

After band class, David's next class was art with Mrs. Iris. She was an older skinny lady, who liked to wear colorful and patterned dresses and big jewelry. On her face she wore big orange glasses, and in her hair she often placed flowers from her garden. Along with her brightly patterned dresses, Mrs. Iris always wore a bright blue apron that was always spotted with paint. She loved her students and was very relaxed when it came to rules. When David walked into the big classroom, he noticed the tables were covered in dry spotted paint from years of being used in the art room. The walls were covered with artwork, and students were everywhere, talking and laughing loudly.

There seemed to be no order in this room, and David couldn't even find Mrs. Iris in the crowd of students. Suddenly, he noticed an older lady walking around passing out blank white T-shirts to the students. When she came to him, she handed him a shirt and continued to go about the room. "Umm, ma'am, are you Miss Iris?" he said, following her around the room.

"That's Mrs., young man," she said, stopping to face him. "I'm glad to meet you. They told me I would be having a new student joining me. Today we are printing on T-shirts some designs we made. I have already instructed the others, so I'm afraid you shall have to sit out for today," Mrs. Iris said sadly; then she went to the front and rang a small bell. The class became silent and attentive as she explained to them the order they would be in to use the printing machine in the back to put artwork on their shirts. David shrugged as he took a seat in the back of the room and stared at the white shirt in his hand.

It wasn't long until he was extremely bored, watching all the other students laughing and designing their shirts. "Hey, look! I found some white fabric paint!" a boy said, searching through the cabinets that sat in the back of the room behind David.

"We're not gonna use white, dude! Our shirts are white!" his friends teased and laughed.

That gave David an idea. Quickly, he stood up and asked, "Can I use that, bro?" to the boy holding the white paint. The boy handed him the paint. David went outside the class, made sure no one was around, and took off his plain black T-shirt and his waistcoat that he was wearing and put on the white shirt Mrs. Iris had given him. He then put his black waistcoat in his backpack to keep it safe. With his black T-shirt in hand, he went back inside and found a large paint brush and some newspaper. He squirted some of the white paint onto the newspaper, dipped his big brush into the paint, and painted a large white cross in the center of his black T-shirt.

"Woah, I wish my shirt was black!" some of the other boys said, seeing his work. David watched the other students taking their finished printed shirts outside to dry. He did the same and after the class was over, his shirt was dry and ready to wear. He put it back on along with his black waistcoat, and returned the plain white shirt to Mrs. Iris after class was dismissed. From then on, David loved to wear shirts with Christian themes and Bible verses on them, but his favorite shirt was always the one he made in art class.

At lunch, David took out of his backpack the lunchbox Mr. Gardien had packed for him and walked over to the tables outside the library. He looked around, holding his metal lunch box, and saw that the tables were all full. He stood searching for a place to sit anywhere, and a loneliness began to fill in his heart once again. Suddenly, he felt a hand touch his shoulder, and he jumped. He turned and saw Abigail holding her lunch tray and smiling. "Want to sit with us?" she asked shyly. Suddenly being confronted by the girl he thought was pretty was a shock, and David found himself mute. All he could bring himself to do was nod yes. "Follow me," she said, heading toward the soccer bleachers.

When they both got there, Moriah greeted them and began asking David many questions about his first day. "How was your first day? Did you like Mr. C? Cool shirt! I like it! Where did you get it? What grade are you?"

"I made it in Art class," he said, looking down at his freshly painted shirt. "I'm in seventh grade, and my first day was all right." David shrugged, trying to remember Moriah's other questions.

"We're in seventh too!" Abby said, taking a bite of her burrito.

"How do you like the teachers?" Moriah asked, sipping her juice.

"They're all cool, except for Miss E. She seems kinda mean," David remarked with a sad expression. Art and Band were David's only fun classes. The rest of the day, he had regular academic classes. English with Mrs. Ante, Math with Miss Garfield, History with Mr. Lincoln, PE with Mr. Ollie. However the hardest of them all was Science with Miss Electron. Her name wasn't really Miss Electron; she called herself that once, and it seemed to stick. All the students agreed she was the meanest teacher in school. A rumor was even started that she once failed a kid for merely sneezing during her lecture.

"I've never had her before," Moriah said, trying to sympathize with David.

"Me neither." Abby shrugged. They decided to change the subject, and they spent the rest of lunch talking about which headphone brand was the best and laughing about what music genre was the worst. The rest of David's day went on fine. Mr. Gardien picked him up after school in his old jalopy and made sure he got all his homework done when they got home. However, they did have a slight disagreement at dinner.

It was late, and David came excitedly into the dining room and sat at the dining room table in the same spot he had sat the night before with his parents. Mr. Gardien placed David's dinner in front of him and went to stand in the corner of the room. "G-man! Dude! Come sit with me!" David whined.

Mr. Gardien answered crossly, "No Mast..., I mean, David. A servant does not dine with his employer."

David paused and stared at his food. He was silent for a few moments; then he raised his head and said to Mr. Gardien, "I read in the Bible that Jesus wants me to serve others, so I'm a servant too. Does that mean you can sit with me now?" Mr. Gardien stared at David with wide eyes for a moment. He didn't answer, but merely smiled with glad eyes. Soon, David became impatient and joked, "I could go get the brooms. We can settle this right here! Right now!"

Mr. Gardien laughed and sighed. "No, David. It has been a long day. I'm too exhausted to argue. I surrender this time. I will go make myself a plate," Mr. Gardien said, going into the kitchen. He returned with a plate of food and a cup of tea for himself, and he sat across from David at the table. When David's parents or a guest would join them at the house, Mr. Gardien would once again stand in the corner and wait on the table. However, when he and David were alone, Mr. Gardien would continue to join David for dinner each night.

CHAPTER 7

NEW BIRTH

Soon, the days passed, and baptism Sunday came before they knew it. David and Abigail signed up to be baptized along with some of the adults in the congregation. The day was crisp and clear. The sun shone brightly, and white puffy clouds coated the sky with beauty. A large pool was brought into the church and placed on the main stage. David, Abigail, and the other new believers all wore thick white robes on top of their underclothes.

Mr. Gardien came to watch David be baptized. He had his old video cassette recorder to record this life-changing moment. Abigail's family was also present. Moriah, as she had already been baptized at age ten, now stood by the baptism pool to support her friends. She also held the mic for the pastor while he was in the pool. Pastor Stanson came up and slowly entered into the pool. Harmoniously, he and the congregation began to pray. Everyone could tell he was nervous; he was always nervous before a baptism. He didn't want to make a mistake on such an important day. Once he was done, the older lady who played the organ began playing the melody of "Amazing Grace." The doors of the church were open. Sunlight broke through, cascading over the line of new believers ready to be baptized. Like a small parade of angels, the line of new believers triumphantly marched into the church. As the pastor had wanted it, David and Abigail were first in line since they were the youngest. "The last shall be first," he told them when they were planning the ceremony.

David looked around in wonder. He couldn't believe this was the same church he had entered in before as an orphaned thief; now he was leaving a child of the Most High God. He looked at the pool as if it were a portal into another world. He slowly put one leg and then the other into the warm water, next to the pastor. The pastor placed his hand on David's shoulder and gently guided him to face the congregation. As David looked at the faces of those around him, he noticed above the church door something he had not seen before. A small stained glass mosaic of Jesus Christ rising from the grave. With a huge smile, Pastor Stanson began to speak into the microphone that Moriah held outside of the pool. "David Raywood, do you believe and trust in Jesus Christ as your Lord and Savior?"

"I do."

"Then upon profession of your faith, I now baptize you in the name of the Father, the Son, and the Holy Spirit." The last thought David had was of his past. The water covered him in heavenly bliss, and the first thing he saw when he emerged was the picture of Jesus's resurrection. Moriah handed him a towel as he stepped onto a plastic sheet that now covered the church floor from water damage. She hugged him and thanked the Lord in that moment for saving David and for having them become friends.

Next was Abigail. She stepped into the pool and stared at all the faces of the people around her. She thought about her past wrongs. She knew she wanted the grace and redemption that only Jesus can give. "Abigail Halieus, do you believe and trust in Jesus Christ as your Lord and Savior?"

"I do."

"Then upon profession of your faith, I now baptize you in the name of the Father, the Son, and the Holy Spirit." The water filled the space around her and made her feel lighter than she had felt in days. Her mind, which was so clouded with regret, suddenly became clearer. As she emerged, a calm and a peace fell over her that she had never known before. As she stepped onto the plastic covering, Moriah quickly handed her a towel and pulled from her back pocket a beautiful golden cross on a silver chain. Abigail was speechless. Moriah put it around her neck and hugged her, thanking the Lord for saving her and for their new best friendship.

The other new believers were also baptized, and the congregation celebrated with cheers and their usual after-baptism church family picnic outside on their front lawn. Abigail and David and the other new believers changed into their clothes. David wore his full three-piece suit because Mr. Gardien let him choose his own clothes, and David knew it would make Mr. Gardien happy. Abigail wore her yellow dress from her aunt and her hair in a ponytail with a yellow ribbon. Tables with red and white checkered tablecloths and plastic chairs were set up with tons of food and drinks. An inflatable bouncy castle was brought in for the children, and some teens were seen playing on it as well. Christian music was being played on a speaker, flying discs were being thrown, balls were being tossed, and games were being played. There was talking, cheering, and laughing all around.

"Catch, Moriah!" Abby laughed, tossing her a flying disc. Cheer was everywhere, except for one sad soul. David and Mr. Gardien sat across from each other quietly at one of the picnic tables. With one hand leaning on the table supporting his cheek, David simply poked at his plate of fried chicken.

"Why are you so melancholy, David? Why aren't you joining in the celebration?" Mr. Gardien asked, concerned. David looked up sadly and pushed his plate away.

"How can I be sure?" David whispered, feeling embarrassed.

"How can you be sure of what?"

"How can I be sure I'm forgiven? How can I be sure I'm saved? What about my past?" David said miserably. Mr. Gardien stared at him a while, with a face that looked like he wanted to say something, but he couldn't.

Finally, Mr. Gardien gave a large sigh and softly asked, "David. Your parents have told me very little about you. What did happen in your past?" David looked at him with wide eyes; then he gave an expression even gloomier than before.

"Well, I never knew my dad. He died before I was born. I was separated from my mom when I was real little. She died in the hospital after we got separated. My brother was eighteen when it happened, and he wanted custody of me. They gave me to him, and he dropped me off at school one day and never came back. I was done with fifth grade when he did that. I haven't seen him since. So I've been on my own, till now." There was silence. With tears in his eyes, Mr. Gardien went over to David and hugged him. They remained like this for a moment.

Then consolingly, Mr. Gardien told him, "I too am a believer, son, and I know the good Lord can use your deepest hurts for His plan. Your birth parents loved you and wanted the best for you, and now the good Lord has forgiven you of your sins because of Jesus's sacrifice. Life spent with Jesus is the best life anyone could ask for." Mr. Gardien paused, gave a sigh, and then continued. "Now, as for your first question about whether you are forgiven. Jesus died to save you, and He Himself said it was finished. Imagine what He suffered; imagine the price He paid. How could such an event not completely save us? Love came down from heaven, died, and rose again so that those who believe in Him are completely redeemed. Jesus Christ suffered and died, not to save you partly but wholly. I know that the good book says that those who are in Him are a new creation. You are not the person you used to be because now you are God's child forever." David felt better, and just in time. For sneaking up behind him were Moriah and Abigail prepared to pull him into the fun. Abigail and Moriah jumped on him and wrapped their arms around his neck, laughing. Then Pastor Stanson came up next to them and took a seat next to David.

Moriah cheered. "Why are you so sad? It is your baptism day!"

"She's right! We're family now. That means we're together, and we are here for you," Pastor Stanson said, patting David on the back.

"It wouldn't be the same without you." Abby smiled.

"Everyone wait just a moment!" Mr. Gardien yelled, jumping to his feet. "Everybody squeeze together! I have always wanted to use my new camera!" Mr. Gardien said, grabbing an old instant photo camera from his video cassette recorder case.

"Yeah, new in the forties," Moriah said, and the teens laughed.

"Say family!" Mr. Gardien said, taking a photo of Abby, Moriah, David, and Pastor Stanson all together. That photo has hung in the hallway, next to David's door, ever since.

That night, David had a nightmare that he had never had before nor that he would ever have again. He dreamed he was in the middle of a deathly dark forest, sitting on a stump of some forgotten dead tree. He was crying, and when he tried to understand why he was crying, he couldn't figure it out. Eerily, red eyes appeared in the dark between the trees, and three creatures crawled out from the darkness. The creatures resembled dark black wolves with horrid, singed wings. They had human hands and feet attached with claws. Two of them walked on all fours and foamed and snarled at the mouth. The third one was much larger than the others, and its wings were much bigger too. It also resembled a black wolf with human hands and feet with claws, but this one walked upright. Its fur was practically completely burned off, and scars were all over its face and arms. The other two creatures on the ground only growled, but the bigger one spoke. In a harsh, grizzly voice, it cursed and raved. It yelled at David in his dream. "Did you really think you could leave me? You're mine. I own you! You're useless! Did you really think He would want you after all you've done? He's the Most High God. You're just a worthless thief! A useless beggar! You'll never lose what you've done!" It went on and on. David couldn't answer the creature; his dream wouldn't let him. It rendered him mute. His dream also wouldn't let him get up from the stump; it wouldn't let him move at all. He wished it would end.

Suddenly, Abigail and Moriah were in his dream. They tore through the trees and were shouting, "Enough! Leave him alone! Stop!" A light was shining brightly from them, and their voices became louder than the creatures.

"David! Don't listen! He's lying! He's trying to trick you and make you fall!" Abby yelled in the dream.

"He who is in Christ is a new creation. You are saved! You are His child! That thing can't touch you!" Moriah yelled in his dream, pointing to the creature. Suddenly, David found himself standing next to Abigail and Moriah against the creature.

He was finally able to speak, and he yelled passionately, "Go away! I am free! I am a child of the Most High God!" The standing creature laughed until it coughed violently. David yelled again, "Jesus Christ is the Son of God! He is Lord over all!" Suddenly, the standing creature growled in anger.

With a horrid wide-open mouth filled with sharp teeth, it shrieked, "Attack them!" The two lesser creatures leaped at the teens. All of a sudden, a light came from above and covered the teens like a bubble. It pushed the creatures back in midleap. The creatures limped away, more singed than before, and the bigger creature howled in pain.

Suddenly, a voice began to call, "David! David! David!"

"David!" Mr. Gardien yelled, shaking him awake. "Wake up! You were having a nightmare! Are you all right?" David hugged Mr. Gardien tight. His heart was beating fast, and he was covered in sweat. He was so frightened.

That Monday was a particularly blustery one. The school day was boring and bleak. When the end-of-lunch bell rang and Abby, David, and Moriah got ready to leave the bleachers and head to their classes, it was just then that David had a very fun idea. "Hey, y'all wanna hang out at..." He paused. David had never invited anyone over to where he lived before, since where he lived before was a crumbling heap. He thought hard for a moment, and he finished with "At my house?" The girls looked to one another to see who would answer first.

Moriah took out her phone and said, "Let me text my dad."

"Yeah, and I'll text my mom," Abby said, getting out her phone.

A moment went by, and since it was time for them to go to their classes, they all three walked a little ways away from the bleachers. Moriah and Abby's phones made a sound, and their parents said yes. "Nice! I'll have Mr. Gardien pick us up after school," David said excitedly. He hurried to his next class, leaving Abby and Moriah alone together.

"Mr. Gardien? Was he the guy at the baptism?" Abigail asked, trying to remember.

"Yes, I thought he was his dad? Oh no! Remember what I told you when I first saw David?" Moriah said nervously.

"You said he was really poor?"

"He must be even poorer than I thought. Maybe Mr. Gardien's his family's financial guardian? Maybe his parents are so poor they need Mr. Gardien to take care of them!"

"That's so sad! Poor guy!" Abby said sadly. "And I thought my parents struggled with money."

After school, David met Moriah and Abby over by the student pickup zone. "You guys all set?" David asked eagerly.

"Certainly," Moriah said with a smile.

"Hey David? You said that Mr. Gardien was gonna pick us up? Who is he?" Abby asked timidly. Moriah nudged her in the side. Before David got there, they had both agreed not to show any type of reaction to David's situation, no matter how poor it might be.

"Mr. Gardien is my guardian. I guess it's about money or whatever." David shrugged.

Moriah gave Abby a look and whispered, "See! I told you so!" Chugging into the pickup zone came Mr. Gardien's old jalopy.

"Hello, little duck, come along! Be a gentleman and help your lady friends into the car here," he called to David from the front seat. David ran over and opened the car's back doors for the girls, and he got into the front seat.

"This is a very nice car," Moriah said, trying to be polite.

"Well thank you, deary. Good to see someone can notice a classic when they see it!" Mr. Gardien said once everyone was inside the car. David rolled his eyes.

The car chugged along, until it came to the Raywoods' large iron gate. When they entered the gate and came in view of the mansion, Abigail and Moriah's jaws dropped. David whirled around in his chair to see their reaction. He laughed and said, "I know, right! I had the same reaction." Moriah and Abby were speechless. The car pulled up close to the Raywoods' front door.

"Here we are." Mr. Gardien sighed, and he and David got out of the car and opened the car doors for the girls.

Before Abby and Moriah stepped out, Abigail nudged Moriah and teased, "Yeah, he's way poorer than we thought!" She giggled, grabbed her backpack, and stepped out of the car. Moriah was stunned and simply kept staring at the mansion in awe. She stepped out slowly, grabbed her backpack, and walked over by Abby and David.

"Yep, this is my house. My parents are away, and Mr. Gardien is my guardian and my parents' butler," David said with a smile. Mr. Gardien went ahead of them and opened the door for them.

"You may enter, Master David and company," he said, standing tall.

David let the girls go in first; then he went over to Mr. Gardien and asked, "G-man. What's up? What are you doing? You know you don't have to be like that around me."

"There's nothing wrong with putting your best foot forward, young man," Mr. Gardien smiled at him and winked. David rolled his eyes and went inside the mansion. Inside, the girls were admiring a rare sculpture by the staircase. David went over to them, and Mr. Gardien came inside.

"Now, I will not have any fiddling with the artwork nor any lolly-gagging about. Come, let us all go into the parlor and enjoy some fresh fruit punch and some of my scrumptious persimmon nut biscuits," Mr. Gardien said, leading the teens past the kitchen and into the Raywoods' large and lavish living room. It was furnished with a long plush velvet couch, two leather arm chairs, a large oak coffee table, and an elaborate fireplace with a roaring fire that could be started with the press of a button. The teens all relaxed on the couch and enjoyed the snacks that Mr. Gardien brought them. They all finished their homework and laughed and talked. It was a wonderfully fun ending to a not so fun day, but it was more than that. Moriah and Abigail didn't treat David any differently than when they mistakenly thought he was still extremely impoverished. They saw him solely as their Christian brother in the faith and their friend.

The next morning, David grabbed his blue backpack and met Mr. Gardien at the front door. "I'm ready!" he said drowsily, and they both hurried out the door to the garage. They both got into Mr. Gardien's old jalopy, and Mr. Gardien turned the key, but nothing happened. The engine didn't start. He tried it again, and still nothing.

"By England's shores, I believe the battery is empty!" Mr. Gardien huffed in frustration.

"What are we gonna do?" David said, hoping Mr. Gardien would say he didn't have to go to school, especially since that day was a test day in science class.

"I shall have to ring your father immediately," Mr. Gardien said, taking out his old flip phone. He exited the car and began a call. David rolled down the window and stuck his head out to listen. "Yes, sir. I understand. Are you perfectly all right with this decision? Very well then, sir. I shall have him there directly," Mr. Gardien said professionally, finishing his call with David's father. Turning to David, he said, "Well, it appears your father wishes for us to use the limousine this turn about."

It was quite an ordeal for Mr. Gardien to try to fit the limousine inside the student drop-off zone, but somehow he did it successfully. If David hated all the eyes staring at him in band class on his first day, he was certainly not prepared for all the eyes that met him as he exited the limo. All of the student body was outside, since the morning bell that signaled for them all to head to class had just rung. Rapidly, a massive crowd of students formed around David. Yesterday he was just another face in the crowd; now he was drawing a crowd. Teens all around him began taking selfies with him, shaking his hand, and attempting to meet him and tell him their names. Many teens attempted to take a photo of the limo before Mr. Gardien drove away. They all assumed David was famous or somebody important that everybody knew. David was shocked and stunned. He just kept smiling and nodding his head as the teens all talked to him.

Suddenly, Valery and her gang approached the crowd. "Everyone move it!" Valery yelled, and the teens closest to her did make room for her. Soon a path was formed, and Valery and her gang walked through the crowd, straight up to David. "Hello, cutie," she said, batting her eyes at him to show off her fake eyelashes. "Nice car! Is it yours?" she asked, getting awkwardly close to him. David wasn't attracted to Valery. David didn't know what to say to her, so he simply stuttered and said, "Uh?" for a long time. He looked to the left and to the right, hoping for a way of escape. Thankfully, Abby and Moriah were waiting for him by the student drop-off zone when the morning bell rang. They saw the limo pull up, and they both figured whose it was. When they saw the crowd overcome David, they knew they had to be the ones to rescue him. They ran over and tried to get to him through the crowd. Their first attempt to reach him failed. Then when Valery made a path, Abby ran over and through the path before it closed again. She made it into the center of the crowd just as Valery had asked David about the car.

"He's not interested," Abby interrupted, getting in between Valery and David.

"Shouldn't you be getting to class?" Valery sneered, shoving Abigail aside to get to David.

"I believe you all should be getting to class," an adult voice commanded above the crowd. It was the principal, who had come out of her office to see what all the commotion was about. All the students paused and looked toward her. One by one they all separated and scattered to their respective classes.

Moriah joined Abby and David as the crowd dissipated. "Thank you. That was super scary," he whispered to them as they headed to their first class of the day.

CHAPTER 8

NATURALLY MUSIC

Fall was just about at its end. October turned into November, and November was moving fast. The leaves turned the colors of gold, brown, red, and orange and fell. Trees became bare, and the wind became cold. Soon, coats and scarfs were being worn in abundance. As the weather outside changed steadily, so did the church's attendance record. Pastor Stanson commented one day that there seemed to be fewer and fewer people attending their Sunday service. "It must be the music? Widow Crewns can't keep playing the organ forever," one of his advisors commented. That is how the search for a new worship leader came about, and that is how David found himself being forced to face one of his greatest fears.

It all started as David, Abby, and Moriah were all hanging out after school at Moriah's house. They were all busy playing a board game in Moriah's living room when Moriah's father came in through the door, looking as if he had just dug a trench. "Woah, Dad! You don't look so well!" Moriah commented, concerned.

"I'll be all right, sweetie. Please bring me a cold ice tea, will you?" her father panted, falling into his old reclining armchair.

Moriah's mother brought out his ice tea just as he had finished asking for it, and she placed it in his hand. "Bad meeting today, dear?" she asked.

"I'll say! If we don't find a new lead vocalist for worship next Sunday, attendance is going to plummet!"

"Why do you need a new vocalist?" Abby asked.

Moriah looked confused. "Yeah, I always thought Ms. Crewns playing the organ was nice."

"She hasn't been enjoying playing the organ for years now. She's been wanting to retire, and now, since we have some room in the budget, she can. We need somebody new. Somebody young and fresh! Pastor Stanson thinks that will bring up attendance." Moriah's father explained. There was a short pause as everyone thought about who could be the new vocalist.

Moriah suddenly began to think out loud, sharing her thoughts with those in the room. "You need somebody young. It would have to be someone with a really nice voice. They would also need to want to attend the church."

"How about you, Moriah?" Abby suggested. "You sing at youth group?"

"Youth group? What's that?" David asked.

"We never told you about youth group? I thought we did! You remember meeting Youth Pastor Andy?" Moriah asked, thinking hard.

David shrugged, "No, I never met any guy named youth pastor. I think I woulda remembered that?"

"Why don't you sing on Sunday, Moriah?" Moriah's mother interrupted, wanting the teens to get back to the topic at hand.

"No way, Mom! I already have to rehearse and learn songs for Wednesdays. Adding Sundays would be way too much! I have school and friends too!" Moriah grumbled. "Besides, didn't you say you wanted someone new? They all have seen me sing before."

"She has a point, darling," Moriah's father commented.

"Well, honey, can you think of anyone else you know who can sing?" her mother asked.

Moriah thought hard for a moment; then her face lit up excitedly. "David!" she shouted, and David was startled and jumped.

"Wha?" he exclaimed, confused.

"David can sing! I saw him sing in band class!"

"David! Why, you're perfect! I'll have to set up an audition for you immediately!" Moriah's father cheered, jumping to his feet and grabbing his coat.

"Hold up! But I don't!" David yelled, but it was too late. Moriah's father was out the door and running to the pastor's office as quick as he could. "Now I know where you get your energy," David teased Moriah, who simply smiled in response.

Next thing David knew, Moriah's father returned in just a few short moments with Pastor Stanson behind him. "David! If you have a moment, come over and audition!" Pastor Stanson asked, smiling. David didn't know what to say. He didn't want to disappoint the pastor. Swiftly, Moriah and Abby stood up and led David by both arms out the door and toward the church. Together they all walked into the church, and David was made to go up onto the stage.

"Come on, lad! Sing us something!" Moriah's father bellowed.

"I don't know how to sing!" David yelled from the stage. "I can't sing!"

"Sure you can! Mr. C said you could, and he teaches music!" Moriah said, coming up on stage and handing David some sheet music. "Here. This is what I was going to sing this Wednesday. Try it out," she said happily. David looked at the sheet music in terror. He had just learned to read a little sheet music, since he had only just begun learning guitar from his tutor. He had a little more than average music experience from his guitar lessons, but there was a special catch in Moriah's father's plan. Being the center of attention was one of David's greatest fears. He hated the thought of people judging him and seeing all the mistakes he may make. Yet there he found himself once again, expected to sing again in front of others. He breathed heavily, and sweat began to pour from his forehead.

They could all tell he was uncomfortable up there, so Moriah's father stood up and said, "How about you help him get more comfortable on stage, Moriah? You can teach him. Let's see. Today is Monday. Let's have you audition on Thursday, David? I'm sure you'll be great!" David jumped off the stage and ran across the room away from it. He had Mr. Gardien pick him up and take him home early from Moriah's house that evening, because he definitely didn't want to sing in front of people ever again.

The next day, Moriah met David after school and asked, "Are you ready for practice?"

"What?"

"You know? Singing practice? For your audition?"

"Look, I never said I was gonna be a singer!" David snapped angrily, "You all just decided for me!" He crossed his arms and turned away from Moriah.

"But Mr. C said you had a great voice!" Moriah pleaded. "Plus you would be doing the church a big favor!" She pressured him and spoke in an earnest voice. David thought about how disappointed the pastor would be if he didn't sing. He thought about Moriah's father possibly not letting him come over anymore. Though these things weren't true in the least, he thought about them just the same. "How about just one practice?" Moriah urged.

"Fine!" David groaned, rolling his eyes. Moriah gave him a hug. When Mr. Gardien pulled up in his jalopy, David asked him to take Moriah and him to the church for singing practice.

"Singing practice?" Mr. Gardien gasped, shocked.

"It's a long story," David moaned, and Mr. Gardien dropped them off at the church. Moriah spent the entirety of two hours training David in singing. She taught him all she could, but David still didn't feel comfortable on stage.

"I know! What you need is experience!" Moriah cheered after their session together was over. "Come and sing with me tomorrow at youth group after your lesson! Then you could get better acquainted with Pastor Andy!" Moriah grabbed her bag and went to go home, but before she could get out the door, David ran up behind her and stopped her.

"Wait!" he said, putting his hand on her shoulder. "I still don't know. What if they laugh at me?"

Turning to face him, she responded, "Laugh at you? You sing great! Why would they laugh at you?"

"Look, I've never sang before!" David yelled in anger. He didn't want to admit to Moriah that he was afraid of singing in public. He was very afraid of sounding bad or looking silly. What he was afraid of most was the others' opinion of him.

Moriah saw he was upset, so she put her hand on his shoulder and said, "Hey, you're going to do fine. Just sing the words on the paper." Then they exited the church. The next day after school, Moriah and David practiced their singing for the youth group meeting that night. He had his guitar, and he was able to play a few chords with the song. Abby came along to their practice this time, and she watched them sing.

When they took a break, she walked over to Moriah and sighed, "You guys look like you're having fun! I wish I could join!"

"Do you play?" Moriah asked while fixing their mic.

"When I was younger, my grandma gave me some piano lessons before she moved away to be with my aunt." Abby shrugged.

"Wait here," Moriah said, and she ran into a side room that was behind the stage. From that room, she dragged out an electric keyboard and its stand. This was a very exceptional keyboard. It had the ability to record live sounds, play them back, and mix the sounds with the rhythm live. It also had the ability to play prerecorded songs and sounds of other instruments. She placed the keyboard on the stand and plugged it into the outlet on stage. Abby went over and warmed up a little. She was a bit rusty, but she did manage to play an extremely simple tune that she had memorized as a child. "That sounds great! Do you think you could play these chords?" Moriah asked as she placed some sheet music in front of the keyboard on a music stand.

Abby asked Moriah to look up the chords on her phone. After reviewing a bit from the internet, Abby was able to play the chords. She practiced it for a while; then she and David tried to play together. He played on guitar and vocals, and they did sync together really well. However, they couldn't start and stop at the same time, and they had some trouble with the beat.

So Moriah had another idea. "How about I go on the drums and count you in?" she suggested, getting out her drumsticks from her backpack. She went over to the drum set on stage and began to play the beginning of the song.

"But how are you gonna sing?" David asked, puzzled.

"Maybe we could give me a mic back here? I'm sure you can sing it on your own now though; you practiced it the entire time at lunch," Moriah smiled. David didn't like that idea, and his breathing became uneasy once again. He jumped off of the stage and ran toward the door. "David!" Moriah yelled, and Abby jumped off the stage after him. Abigail was the fastest runner in school, and she easily caught up to David outside the church and got in front of him.

"What's wrong?" she asked, stopping him midstride.

"I don't wanna sing! I don't wanna embarrass myself up there," he said, turning away from her. "Why do they even want me to anyway?" David sulked and sat down on the alleyway steps between building one and two. Abigail took a seat next to him, and they were both silent for a while.

Abby coughed; then she quietly stated, "Why do you want to?"

"I don't want to!"

"Why?"

"I just told you! They'll all laugh at me! I'm gonna look so...I don't know!" David yelled.

"Do you sing in church?"

"Yeah? I don't mind that! 'Cause everybody else around you is singing."

"What if you were alone?" Abby asked seriously.

"Sure, whatever. I wouldn't mind singing alone. That's not the point."

"So what you're saying is you are a different person when you're alone than when you're in public?"

"No? But I'm embarrassed when I'm on stage."

"Cause you're worshipping the Lord?"

"No! 'Cause of my singing!"

"You have a wonderful voice! If they didn't think so, they wouldn't have chosen you! It doesn't matter what anyone else thinks anyway. What matters is what the Lord thinks, and if you can worship Him alone, nothing should change when you're on stage."

David thought about this a minute, but he still wasn't satisfied. "What if they don't like me? What if people leave the church because I make a mistake on stage?"

"Does the Lord want you to worship Him?" Abigail asked in a serious tone. David rolled his eyes because he knew the Lord would. David realized that what Abigail said was true and that if the Lord wanted him to do it, then there was no other argument. He thought about her words, and how it was true that only what the Lord thought of him mattered. If the Lord was pleased with him, that was what counted. That meant it didn't matter if people liked him or not. It only mattered if he was doing what the Lord wanted him to do. He thanked her; then David and Abby stood up and marched back into the church.

Moriah was sitting on the stage, thumbing through her Bible. "David! I found a passage I think you will like! It has to do with King David! It's 2 Samuel chapter six! It's about King David dancing before the Lord after the Ark of the Covenant was brought into—"

"You're gonna tell me I should focus on what the Lord thinks and not what anyone else thinks." David smiled, interrupting Moriah.

"I just like that passage. Why? Are you better now?"

"For sure, and I'll totally check that out later! Can you text it to me? But I got to go do somethin' real quick," David said, heading out the door. Outside alone, he prayed to the Lord and asked the Lord to renew his strength and his heart. David went back inside and jumped onto the stage. Moriah counted them in, and together they played well.

That night, David walked into the youth group room, his heart beating fast. Pastor Andrew had just finished setting up Moriah's drums, Abby's keyboard, and David's microphone. "So here's the famous singer. Moriah told me you have a great voice. I can't wait to hear it, bro!" the pastor said, giving him a fist bump. David liked him immediately. Nervously, David went up to the front and waited for Abby and Moriah to get there. Soon, Abigail and Moriah came in and joined him up front. Together they played a rendition of a modern worship song about not turning back from following Jesus Christ. They were nervous, but the Lord moved in all of them, and their song was filled with the power of the Holy Spirit and with Truth. Throughout the entire song, David focused on what the Lord thought of him, and his nervousness melted away with every note. The next day was David's audition for the position of the church's lead vocalist. He prayed that morning for the Lord's will to be done with the decision.

After that, the Lord, through His Holy Spirit, put it on David's heart for him to turn down the audition and called him to a slightly different position. So David walked in for his audition and went up to Pastor Stanson and Moriah's father and said, attempting to stand tall, "Sirs, I can't be your worship singer."

Moriah's father gasped. "What! I thought we had gone through this! Are you still afraid to sing?"

"Let's hear the boy out, John," Pastor Stanson said, calming him down.

"No I'm not afraid to sing Mr. MacAaron, but I don't want to sing on Sundays. I want to sing at youth group. I feel that is where the Lord is calling me, to support and play with my friends," David bravely replied.

Pastor Stanson laughed and joked at Moriah's father, "That youth group's taking all your talent, John." Then, the pastor gave a serious look as he did when he was trying to understand something difficult. "Now who are we going to find to lead worship? I already told Widow Crewns she could retire from playing the organ, and she was so happy," he said thoughtfully, beginning to pace about. Moriah's father and David also became thoughtful. They stood around and thought and thought for quite some time.

"You know, I haven't heard a choir sing in ages," Moriah's father commented. The pastor paused midpace, stood still for a moment, and then turned to Moriah's father in excitement.

"Splendid! A choir! We could invite members from the congregation to join! We could find a room in building one for them to rehearse, and we could hire a choir director!" the pastor said excitedly, leading Moriah's father away and out the door as they talked. Alone in the church, David stared up at the cross that hung above the pulpit. With a smile, he thanked the Lord and headed out the door into the daylight.

CHAPTER 9

A LIGHT UPON A HILL

Before anyone could imagine it, November turned into December. Snow had not yet fallen, but the weather was extremely cold. As David, Abby, and Moriah were passing the church all bundled in their coats, they noticed Pastor Stanson bringing out the outdoor Nativity scene pieces and randomly placing them out on the church lawn. "Uh? Pastor? I don't know if you know this, but that isn't how it goes," Moriah teased. They all laughed.

The pastor responded sarcastically, "Ha ha. Very funny. Actually, I believe you three could really help me. I need some willing volunteers to help me set these statues up. What do you say?"

"Sure," David said, picking up a lamb statue from the lawn.

"But, pastor? We just got done with the fall festival? Isn't it a little early for the Nativity?" Abby asked, moving the wise men together in a row.

"I know very well what time it is. I just thought that since this Nativity is a symbol of the love of God, it is something that we should celebrate no matter what time of year it is!" Pastor Stanson snapped angrily. The teens all became silent because they knew they had struck a nerve. "I'm sorry, kids. I've just been so busy lately. Always during this time of year, it seems people are coming out of the woodwork to ask things from me. I'm feeling very worn down," the pastor said, trying to pick up one of the camel statues.

"I know, right! I'm feeling like that too!" David groaned, running over to help him with the camel statue. "Mr. Gardien and I've been busy giving to charities and volunteering and stuff all over the place. We're runnin' everywhere!"

"My backpack's gonna make me fall one of these days! We get way, way, way too much homework!" Abby moaned, placing a staff in a shepherd's hand. David and Moriah both nodded their heads in agreement with Abby.

"Same! Ms. E's been pilin' it on!" David grumbled.

"My homework load seems tripled! My dad's been busy too! Coat drives, shoe drives, food drives! He has been fundraising nonstop!" Moriah griped. Everyone around that Nativity agreed that they were all extremely busy. So busy in fact, that they all seemed tired and overwhelmed, but this was only the beginning of the teens' stress levels rising.

At the teens' middle school, there came a great controversy that swept over the entire campus. One group of boys who were the regular bullies in the school was having some trouble with one of its members.

One of the members liked Azul from Valery's clique, and none of the boys from that group were supposed to like girls from Valery's gang because Valery and her gang hated sports. Soon, rumors about their secret relationship began to grow. From ridiculous stories to eyewitness accounts, the rumors got bigger and more hurtful as they grew. Soon, the students began picking sides about which rumors were true and which ones weren't, and this started fights all throughout the school, all because these two were supposed to be from groups that hated each other. This caused tension and strife all around David, Moriah, and Abigail. Every day, people would ask them whose side they were on and what they thought of the matter, but none of them wanted to fight about it. They knew gossiping about others behind their backs was something the Lord didn't want them to do. They all three resolved to stay quiet about the matter, but this brought them nearer and nearer into the spotlight. Before long, students began to talk and wonder why David, Abby, and Moriah wouldn't join in the rumors and the gossip. Rapidly it was spreading that perhaps Moriah, Abby, and David knew something about the rumors that only they three knew, and the spotlight turned on them. Everyone around them began watching them closely and pressuring them to say why they weren't joining in the gossip. No matter what David, Abby, and Moriah told the other students about them wanting to listen to the Lord, it didn't satisfy the gossip-hungry crowd, and the others accused the three teens of stalling, covering up, or not telling the truth. This made David, Moriah, and Abigail angry, on edge, and stressed to the max.

Finally, the weekend came, and they could finally be away from school. Moriah texted Abby and David and suggested they go to the movies to watch the newest cartoon film. They all agreed, and they all met outside the closest movie theater to buy tickets. "This is going to be so fun!" Moriah cheered.

"I know, right! This movie looks totally cute, and like, it's so nice to be away from all that drama." Abby laughed.

"I'll get the tickets, my treat!" David shouted when they got up to the ticket window. Suddenly, a loud moan came from behind them, and they all three paused and turned around.

"Well if it isn't the cutie and his entourage," Valery jeered at them. She and her clique were all in line to buy tickets for the same movie.

"'Cause of you three, this whole thing with Azul is still happening!" Brunhilda yelled at them.

"What are you talking about?" Abby asked annoyed.

"Don't you check Face-novel? Everybody wants to know why you guys haven't joined in the conversation," Bertha said, continuously texting on her phone.

"Yeah, it was about Azul and what's his name. Now it's about you three, and it won't end till you guys spill!" Gretchen smirked accusingly, beginning to film Abby, Moriah, and David with her phone as if expecting a confession.

"We only want to know why you haven't been caring about the fight." Dorcus shrugged.

"Look, we just want to watch the new movie. So, could you hurry this up?" Valery whined, gesturing for David to buy the tickets. Abigail knew that if there were rumors to be made, Gretchen would be the one to make them. She didn't want to sit in the theater with the pressure of Gretchen behind them, watching their every move, and she didn't put it past Valery to ask Bertha to record them while they sat, in order to find some incriminating evidence on them later.

"Guys, I think I don't wanna watch this movie right now after all," she said sadly.

"Me neither," Moriah moaned. She had been thinking the same things.

"Let's just go hang out in the youth group room," David said, and they all walked away from the theater and down the street, heading toward the church. As they walked, they all felt their stress levels rising. School, homework, Valery, sports, church, family, youth group, friends, and everything else they had on their minds was almost too much to handle. "I wish there was a place we could get away." David sighed as they walked along.

"Maybe there is?" Abby said, stopping abruptly. She paused and looked over to the right. David and Moriah walked a few steps forward before they realized she had stopped. When they realized she wasn't behind them anymore, they both joined her. Sitting exactly in the middle of their square-shaped community, at the center of everything, rising above all the buildings in the area, was a large grassy hill. "We could have a picnic!" Abby shouted. Moriah and David both thought this was a great idea. They all hurried home to ask their parents and guardian for permission and to pick up supplies.

"Isn't it foul weather to be having a picnic?" Mr. Gardien commented to David as David ran and opened the nearest closet to grab some pillows and a big blanket. "The forecast said snow was to come in a few more days?"

"We'll have big coats on, and this'll be fun! It won't be that bad!" David said, rushing toward the door with his supplies. He thanked Mr. Gardien and rushed toward the grassy hill. Moriah and Abby's parents commented similar sentiments, but the teens didn't mind the weather. They just wanted to have some fun alone. They all rushed up the hill, as quickly as they could. Moriah brought a picnic basket filled with sandwiches and snacks. Abby brought some thermoses filled with hot chocolate, and David brought a blanket and some pillows. They all sat cold but comfortable on top of that hill. The view was incredible. The teens could see for miles all the way around. Buildings and cities hundreds of miles away could be seen clearly, and their own little town was laid before them clear as day. The sky seemed to never end, and the teens imagined the clouds could touch the tops of their heads. They all enjoyed the quiet and the tranquility up there. Their thoughts seemed to become clearer, and their spirits were lighter with the sound of laughter and silence in plenty. After they finished eating, they all laid down on the blanket and stared up at the sky. The silence lasted for quite a while, and for the first time in a long time, they all were able to hear themselves think. In the silence, the teens found it easier to focus on God and His Word. Far away from every distraction, each one of the teens prayed to God in their hearts and concentrated their thoughts on verses from the Bible.

It was very beneficial to them and lasted quite a while until Moriah spoke up. "It says in the Psalms, 'Be still and know that I am God.' I think this place is great for that."

"Maybe that's what we need to do more often. Just rest in knowing that He is God. Maybe then we wouldn't be so stressed," Abby said, stretching out on the blanket.

"Sounds right to me. When I think of God, the things I'm stressed about don't seem as big," David added with a yawn.

"Wouldn't it be great if we could shout the gospel from this height?" Abby thought out loud. Rapidly, Abigail sat up and shouted "Hey! I've got an idea!"

Once they had cleaned up and packed up their picnic, the teens all hurried down to the city hall where all their communities' records were kept. "Who owns the big hill over there?" David asked the city clerk.

The man straightened his bow tie and said in a squeaky voice, "I am sure we do, young man. Now run along, unless you were planning on donating your milk money to the city council." The man laughed hysterically at his own joke.

David and Abby went to leave, but Moriah remained by the counter and yelled, "Yeah. David Raywood! Let's go!" before she turned and walked away briskly.

"Why did you use my full name?" David whispered.

"Shh!" Moriah pushed him forward.

"Wait! David Raywood? You're the son of Mr. and Mrs. Raywood?" the clerk gasped. David turned around and nodded his head yes. "I was not aware that they had any children. Prove it!" the clerk dared, looking at David suspiciously. David took out his phone and showed the man a picture of him and his parents at the dinner table on the first night they met. Next thing the teens knew, they were being brought into the restricted records room of the city hall. "This is where you'll find the records you're looking for, Mr. Raywood. I hope it is all to your satisfaction," the clerk said, standing like Mr. Gardien does when David's parents are in the room.

"Thanks, dude! This is sick!" David said excitedly. The clerk gave a look of shock, and David coughed and quickly added, "I mean, that will be all." The clerk left the room, and the teens all giggled and smiled as they began opening file cabinets and looking through old documents. After many record books were opened and many files skimmed through, Moriah, who loved history, finally found something along the lines of their search.

"Look at this!" she shouted, holding an old black and white photo of a small white building sitting atop the hill. "This pic came with this," Moriah said, showing Abby and David an official document, sealed and stamped with an official letterhead. "It says here, that…" Moriah read and paused in order to finish counting in her head. "Ninety years ago, the church was first built on that hill! I wonder why they moved?"

"I guess we could ask Pastor Stanson. Maybe he knows," David suggested.

"The church sits at the base of the hill now. Weird!" Abby commented as they left the record room. They ran over to the church and went up the stairs of building one to Pastor Stanson's office. They knocked on the door, and he welcomed them in. He looked very tired. Piles of papers and bills were stacked high on his desk. His phone was unplugged and thrown in the trash. From these signs, the teens guessed he was probably not having a very pleasant Saturday.

"What can I do for you? I'm afraid this consultation will have to be quick. I have a meeting with the choir director in fifteen minutes. Then I have a budget meeting with my secretary, and I have to approve posters for the bake sale." The pastor's grumbling became a series of angry mumblings too low for the teens to hear.

"We're sorry to disturb you. We were just wondering how come the church moved from the top of the hill in the center of town to the bottom, and does the church still own it? Because we have an idea we would like to try," Moriah asked politely.

Pastor Stanson paused from looking through his papers and stared at Moriah intensely. "I see," he said, sitting back in his armchair and breathing a deep sigh. "Well, what happened is plainly this. We had to move the church to the base of the hill because some of our older members with walkers and some of our members in wheelchairs couldn't make it up that big hill any longer. I know that going up that steep hill doesn't seem hard for strong young ones like yourselves, but with my knees I couldn't even make the trek up that hill now," the pastor laughed; then he got up and went over to his file cabinet. He slowly bent down to the bottom drawer, opened it, and thumbed through his files to the back of the drawer. "Here we go!" he said, taking out an old file and blowing the dust off of it. "If I understand it correctly, we still own that hill," he said, opening the file on his desk. "Here, see! Here's the proof in black and white," Pastor Stanson said, handing them an official proof of ownership for the hill. The teens all grinned from ear to ear.

"Awesome! 'Cause we have an idea that we think you're gonna like!" David said excitedly.

"We just had some silent time with God, sir, and we feel really refreshed! Maybe you could take a break and join us up there one day?" Abigail added.

"I don't think my knees would make the trip up that hill now. However, you young ones go ahead. A break in my office does sound wonderful, little missy," the pastor sighed in his chair.

A few hours later, David, Abigail, and Moriah were on top of the hill with one long piece of wood and one short piece of wood. They also brought a shovel, a hammer, nails, and rope. David dug a hole right in the center of the top of the hill. The girls nailed the short piece of wood horizontally across the long piece of wood. They tied rope onto either side of the short piece, and together they all pulled the whole thing into the hole, and once it sat up straight, David refilled the hole. They had made a cross, a symbol of God's great sacrifice, for all the town to see on top of their peaceful and beautiful hill. Just as they finished, God created an extra beautiful sunset that night, and they watched as colors of purple, orange, red, and yellow exploded in the sky behind their cross. The last beams of sunlight blasted through the night and outlined the cross in beautiful light. The next morning, everyone in town noticed the cross, and so did all the students at Lancer Middle

School. They all were so busy wondering who had built the giant cross that they all forgot to gossip about Azul and the boy. Soon those rumors died out, and as soon as they did, everyone stopped staring at and pressuring David, Abby, and Moriah. From then on, when any of those three felt stressed, they would go up the hill and spend some time sitting at the foot of the cross, being still, and knowing who is, was, and will always be forever God.

CHAPTER 10:

THE FOURTH IS ADDED

That month of December was filled with stories that the teens will always remember, but that is for another time. The snowy months of December and January passed swiftly. Before long, the flowers began to awake from their prolonged slumber. The trees regrew luscious green leaves, and the birds began to sing new songs full of hope and joy. One particularly bright and sunny day in the beginning of March, David, Abigail, and Moriah were strolling down the sidewalk heading toward the church in order to practice their music for Wednesday's youth group service. They were just returning from dropping Abigail's siblings off at her house and were debating about what songs they should sing when they heard a loud thud, as of many objects falling, across from them on the other side of the street. They all exchanged worried looks, and David ran ahead a few paces to see what had happened. Across the street on the adjacent sidewalk, he saw a group of older high school boys in a circle, surrounding a young man that looked to be his age. At the feet of the young man in the center were books scattered all around. He had a full head of wavy brown hair. On his face, he wore glasses with black frames, and on his person, he wore jeans, a white collared shirt, and a horizontal striped yellow and brown sweater over his shirt. David ran over to the scene, with Abigail and Moriah not far behind. When David and the girls got there, it didn't take them long to see this was a bullying situation.

"Leave him alone!" David yelled at the older boys, stopping and crossing his arms at them. There were four tough older boys surrounding the younger one. The four older boys were known to the local high school as the school's resident bullies, but to these middle schoolers, that was unknown to them. Though if they had known it, they wouldn't have changed their actions. The thirteen-year-old boy in the center of the vicious circle stared straight up at the bullies with a serious expression, not budging an inch.

"Get outta here, middle schoolers! Go play on the swing set!" the toughest bully laughed as he stared down the thirteen-year-old boy in the center intensely. "What you gonna do about it, little guy?" the bully laughed along with his assailants. Like the climax scene of a movie with a ticking time bomb, the tension was rising. No one was quite sure what was going to happen next. Everyone held their breath. Suddenly, Moriah marched up, past David, right into the center of the circle of bullies.

She bravely stood next to the thirteen-year-old boy, placed her hand on his shoulder, and quietly whispered, "We'll help you pick up your books." She bent down and began picking up the books. David and Abigail saw what she was doing, and they both ran in and joined her. The young man was shocked and quickly got down with them and began helping and was handed all his books. "I love these titles. They really are quite fascinating. My name is Moriah," Moriah said, shaking hands with the young man.

"My name is Jonathan," he said quietly. Once Jonathan had most of his books in hand, and Moriah, David, and Abigail had the rest, they all stood to their feet. The bullies, seeing that the odds were now four against four, didn't want to cause Jonathan anymore trouble, but they also didn't want to look weak in their own minds either.

So the roughest bully scoffed. "Yo, you need a stupid pint-sized girl to fight your battles little guy?"

"Don't speak about her like that!" Jonathan ordered seriously at the bully.

"Oh yeah? Well what if we teach you and your friends here some manners? What you gonna do then?" the bullies laughed, taking a step closer to Jonathan and Moriah.

Jonathan, speaking rather quickly, responded, "I'm going to quickly increase my levels of adrenaline, engage my hamstrings, quadriceps, and calf muscles, speedily adhere the bottom surface area of the soles of my feet with the surface area of the concrete and increase my forward momentum heading northeast."

"What? What did he say?" the bullies said, exchanging confused looks with one another.

"In other words, run!" Jonathan shouted, grabbing Moriah's hand and running speedily away from the scene. David and Abigail followed quickly behind. The bullies were so confused that they didn't even chase after the teens. The middle schoolers all ran through street after street until they were sure they were safe. Before long, they were walking easily again, and they laughed and talked with their new friend. They all decided that since it would be dark soon and too late to rehearse by the time they made it back to the church, they thought it would be a good idea to help their new friend carry his books home. After walking down a couple of side streets, they made it to Jonathan's two-story, four-bedroom home, and David, Moriah, and Abigail handed him his books, and he placed them in his moss green and brown backpack.

"Wow! I know this street! I pass it on the way home! You live half a block from me! We're like neighbors!" David cheered, high-fiving Jonathan.

"And I don't live far away either, and neither does Moriah." Abby beamed.

"So you're going to join our school tomorrow?" Moriah asked, clarifying their earlier conversations.

"That is correct. My parents and I just moved here from my aunt's house a few towns over. Approximately a month ago, we came to this country from Israel. Thank you for helping me carry my books and helping me against those bullies," Jonathan finished saying with an eye roll. The teens all said they were glad to do it, smiled, and waved goodbye to each other. They had to make sure they all made it home for dinner.

The next day, as David stood outside of his science class with the rest of his classmates, Miss Electron came walking up, late as usual, with her large coffee mug in her hand. Her hair was in a tightly wrapped bun that sat on top of her head like a tiny brown hat. She wore very old-fashioned clothing, with long lace sleeve shirts that covered her entire neck and long black skirts and dresses that were so long that they covered her feet and even draped a little behind her. With a tired groan, she haphazardly found her keys in one of her skirt pockets and unlocked the classroom door. "I needed my coffee; it makes me nicer," she muttered as her students entered the class.

"If this is her nice, I would hate to see what she's like when she's not nice." One student snickered with another, and Miss Electron slammed the class door in response. The students all ran quickly to their seats and sat up straight in fear. David was the only one who relaxed in his seat in the back of the room. The class was filled with many small tables that sat two students per desk. David was the only one in the room who did not have a table partner. After sipping her coffee from her mug, Miss Electron picked up her famous ruler and slammed it onto her teacher's desk up in the front.

She spoke in a serious, almost threatening tone. "Now, I'm sure you are all aware that the school board demands that I incorporate some form of creativity within our study of the course of biology. So I will be assigning you a group project this afternoon, not unlike the ones you have already completed previously in the school year." The students all moaned and complained out loud, forgetting whose class they were in. Miss Electron slammed her ruler upon the desk once again, and the students sat up straight and silent once more. "You will be working with your table partners to complete this assignment. Together you will each—" Miss Electron was interrupted by a knock at her classroom door. She hastily went over and swung the door wide open. Outside stood Jonathan, holding his class schedule in his hand.

"Hello, ma'am, I am new here, and the office told me I am assigned to this class," he said kindly, but Miss Electron didn't like to be interrupted.

"Come in, find a seat, and be quiet," she ordered, returning to her spot in the front. Jonathan walked slowly in, closed the door, and found the seat next to David.

"Don't worry, she's that way with everyone," David whispered and chuckled with Jonathan.

Miss Electron slammed her ruler on her desk once again. "Since we seem in a chatting mood, I have decided we will review last night's reading before I introduce you to your new project." Her eyes narrowed in on David. The students all gave looks of disgust, reached into their backpacks, and took out their homework from last night. Miss Electron opened her teacher's textbook and read the first question out loud, "What does DNA stand for?" The students all had blank expressions on their faces. Jonathan raised his hand high in the air, and Miss Electron called on him.

"Deoxyribonucleic acid," he stated matter-of-factly. Everyone in the room was surprised, including Miss Electron. The students all began to gasp and whisper quietly about Jonathan.

Not wanting to lose her students' attention, Miss Electron quickly read the next question. "What is a cell?" This time several other hands sprang up along with Jonathan's. Miss Electron, out of curiosity, chose to call on Jonathan once again.

"It is extremely tiny, and it is what science has concluded animals and plants are made of," he said happily.

"How are you getting these? You didn't even do the homework, man!" David gasped. He accidently said this comment a little too loud, and Miss Electron's eyes narrowed in on him again.

Miss Electron practically growled at David, "Well, Mr. Raywood. Since you are in such a talkative mood this afternoon, then you must be willing to answer the next question from the reading." David stammered and looked down at his homework, hoping earnestly that he was going to be able to answer her correctly. Miss Electron, wanting to make an example out of David, searched in her teacher's textbook for the hardest question she could find.

"How many layers are there in a plant cell wall?" she asked triumphantly. She knew there was no way David could answer her since this question came from material she had not covered yet, either in class or in the reading. She smiled proudly as she watched David's eyes widen.

"Uh?" he began, unsure of the answer. He stared at his homework anxiously. Suddenly Jonathan's hand slowly moved along the top of the desk and landed in David's peripheral view. Quickly, he secretly showed David a number three with his fingers. David understood what was happening and quickly said out loud, "Umm? Three?" Miss Electron's eye's widened. It didn't take her long to figure out why her plan didn't work and swiftly she turned her angry stare on Jonathan.

"Young man, please allow your fellow students to reach the correct answers on their own," she said crossly, slamming her textbook closed. When she turned around to the board, Jonathan and David fist-bumped. Miss Electron shouted, "Pass your homework to the left, and if they are not collected and brought up to my desk in five minutes, they will all be docked five points." Panic ensued as the students threw their papers to each other and the student most to the left of the room raced frantically to collect all the papers and run them to Miss Electron's desk. The student made it with one minute to spare. Miss Electron snarled as she repulsively skimmed through the papers. She placed them down on her desk aggressively and began to write on the board once again. "Now, I will introduce you to your new group project. Together with your table partner you will be creating a three-dimensional model of an animal cell with a written guide on what parts are which, and each part shall be labeled. This will be my fourth year of grading these repetitive, odious reproductions. So this year I am adding a new stipulation. Your models must be artistic and creative. The model that is the most creative will earn ten extra credit points." All the students cheered and began to dream about what their grade would look like if they won those extra credit points.

"That means we are doing this together, right?" Jonathan asked David excitedly.

"Yeah, and I gotta get those points!" David said passionately. He had failed the last test, and those extra points would really help his grade.

"How about you come over to my house, and we can get started on it tonight?" Jonathan cheered.

David nodded his head and smiled, "Yeah! Cool dude!"

At lunch, Jonathan, with his homemade bag lunch in his hand, stood alone in the center of all the hustle and bustle that lunchtime in a middle school typically creates. As he stood, wondering where to sit, David came up behind him and tapped him on the shoulder. "Hey!

Wanna sit with us?" David asked with a smile. Jonathan nodded yes, and together they walked to the bleachers. There Abby and Moriah greeted him with a hug and two bright big smiles. They all laughed, talked, and really enjoyed their time together.

Later that day, David cheerfully walked down the block toward Jonathan's house with his school backpack on his shoulders, now filled with his silk pajama shirt and pants, toothbrush, and many other essentials needed when one spends the night at another's house. In both hands, he held a large plastic tub containing the materials Jonathan had texted and asked him to bring. Happily, David walked up the walkway of Jonathan's house and knocked on the door. Jonathan's mother answered the door warmly. "David! Shalom! It is a pleasure to meet you! Welcome!" She shook his hand and welcomed him inside.

"Thank you. Is Jonathan here?"

"Yes, Jonathan's room is up the stairs, to the left." David thanked her and ascended the stairs excitedly. Once his foot had left the last step, he turned and faced a door covered in space stickers. Greeted by stickers of planets, astronauts, stars, and rocket ships, David softly knocked on the door. He knew this had to be Jonathan's room because Jonathan had mentioned to him that he was an only child.

"Come in!" Jonathan called from inside. David entered, and he looked around the room. From one side of the door, extending across two walls, was a continuous shelf that was waist high. Chaotically scattered on this shelf, were papers, pens, pencils, and open journals and textbooks galore. Neatly labeled jars filled with curious powders, bizarre objects, and strange chemicals lined the back of this shelf.

Microscopes, test tubes, flasks, beakers, and hot plates lay sporadically across the shelf along with various hand tools, wires, nuts, bolts, and strange pieces of metal. In the corner of the room, where the two shelves connected, sat a large globe of the world and a large telescope that pointed out of Jonathan's huge circular bedroom window. Against one of the walls without any shelving was Jonathan's space-themed bed, and next to that, on the other wall, was a large whiteboard with long complicated math equations written out on it in marker. On the walls above the waist-high shelving hung posters of star constellations and famous rocket launches. David took a step further into the room, heard a crunch sound, and saw he had stepped on a crumbled paper ball. The floor was covered in crumbled paper balls and empty crushed root beer cans. David looked up and saw that Jonathan's ceiling was covered in glow in the dark sticker stars.

"You really like science stuff, huh?" David gasped, admiring the stars on the ceiling. Jonathan, sitting atop a rolling stool and dressed in his safety goggles, lab coat, and gloves, was too preoccupied with a chemistry experiment to answer. Slowly, he took a dropper and carefully placed it into one of his beakers. He sucked up a couple drops of the strange chemical within the beaker, carried the dropper over to another full beaker that sat on top of one of his hot plates, cautiously dropped a few precious drops of the chemical one by one into the beaker, and watched as the reaction fizzed and bubbled.

"Yes! Satisfactory!" he mumbled to himself as he wrote down some notes into one of his open journals.

"I brought the art stuff you wanted. Should I put it here?" David asked gesturing to a spot on Jonathan's messy shelf.

"Magnificent! You may place it there," Jonathan said, standing to his feet and taking off his lab coat, goggles, and gloves. He simultaneously grabbed for what appeared to be a big metal box with wheels, an antenna, and a wireless remote controller. He placed the box on the floor and began controlling it with the remote control. "Sorry about the mess. I'll have it cleaned in no time," he said, playing with the remote controller and leading the small robot over the crumbled paper balls and crushed cans of root beer. As the box moved along the ground, it sucked up the trash wherever Jonathan told it to go.

"You made that?" David gasped, placing the tub of art supplies he had been holding on the shelf and watching as the little robot zoomed around.

"Certainly. Building robots is my hobby. Along with dabbling in experiments, chemistry, biology, and stuff." Jonathan smiled.

"Can I try?" David asked, gesturing to the remote.

"Sure," Jonathan said, handing David the remote and going to investigate the tub of art supplies. As David enjoyed maneuvering the box robot, Jonathan searched inside the tub. "This is great! Now all we have to do is judiciously decide how to make our cell model extremely creative."

"I like art stuff," David commented while playing with the robot.

Jonathan leaned up against his shelf and made the face he normally makes when he is thinking very hard about something. "Let's see. It will need to be spherical to some degree and contain all the average organelles of the cell, the nucleus and so on."

"What if we drew an awesome picture of it?"

"Can't. She said it had to be three dimensional, remember?" Jonathan said sadly.

"Oh yeah! True!" David said, distracted by the robot.

"Well, I suppose we should start by finding something spherical that we could cut in half to start with. The others might use a foam ball from the craft store, but we could try something else?" Jonathan suggested, picking up the robot from the floor once David had told it to pick up the last bit of trash.

David handed Jonathan the remote and agreed. "Yeah, but where we gonna find that?"

"Let's look in my basement," Jonathan suggested as he hurried over and ran out of the room and down the stairs. David quickly followed, and together they hastily headed down to Jonathan's basement stairs.

CHAPTER 11

NEW TREASURES AS WELL AS OLD

"I don't know about this. Hanging out in people's basements ain't exactly very fun for me," David commented as they entered Jonathan's basement.

"Do not be nervous. My parents keep our basement very neat and organized almost like another room of the house. My parents are archeologists and have collected many valuable artifacts from all around Israel," Jonathan explained, turning on the basement light. David was shocked to see that Jonathan was right. The basement's walls were stacked very neatly with boxes labeled and categorized according to size. On the floor was carpeting, and in the center of all the boxes was an extremely long table. David looked around the basement with immense curiosity. On the wall hung a large map of Israel, and below this map was a long shelf that held square glass cases like ones you might find in a museum. David examined the map and stared up at the glass cases. Inside he saw fragments of very, very old documents written in ancient Hebrew along with pieces of ancient artifacts that must have been around for longer than David could imagine. Each artifact and fragment sat on a velvet pillow, carefully preserved.

He stared and walked parallel along the shelf, admiring each glass case individually, until he came to an artifact that didn't have a case or a pillow. It sat by itself on the shelf with glass cases on either side of it. It appeared to be an old, worn leather strap and pouch. Since it didn't have a case, David assumed it was okay to touch it. He picked it up gently and brought it to Jonathan who was busy searching in one of the boxes. "What's this, dude?" David asked, showing Jonathan the leather strap.

Jonathan shrugged. "Oh, that's a replica of the slingshot King David might have used when he fought the philistine Goliath. My father accidently knocked down its case, and we have not bought a new one yet."

David gasped. "Wait, you're telling me King David used this slingshot?"

"He might have used one like it, to the best of our knowledge."

"And you haven't played with it yet!" David yelled excitedly.

"I did when I was little. Here let me show you," Jonathan said, taking the pouch from David's hand. He swung it around in a circle very fast. David's excitement grew immensely, and a big grin was on his face. When Jonathan finished his demonstration, he walked the slingshot back to its place on the shelf and explained, "If this sling was really as old as it is pretending to be, I could not use it, but it's made of new materials, new leather, and just made to look old."

David was extremely fascinated by the slingshot, but he knew that they had to continue working if they wanted to find a sphere for their science project. So David meandered over to another part of the basement, and he noticed that on the long table there was placed an unrolled scroll of white wax paper, and placed on this wax paper was a small stone with engraving on it. "Hey, Jonny, what's this?"

"Don't call me Jonny," Jonathan called, walking away from looking into one of the boxes. He strolled over and smiled. "That is one of my parents' favorite finds. They have not been able to date it thus far. My parents have been very busy working at the downtown history and science museum, helping them to take care of their ancient documents."

"What's it say?" David asked, admiring the carving on the stone. Jonathan turned on the lamp that sat close to the table and discerningly peered at the stone. Next to the stone was a bundle of papers with his mother's handwriting on them. The light was bright above the table as David stood with Jonathan, looking at the ancient Hebrew written on the stone. Jonathan's attention turned from the stone to his mother's translation of the ancient Hebrew into a better readable version on her notes. Jonathan began to read the ancient text in Hebrew. Hearing Jonathan speak Hebrew fascinated David, and he listened respectfully. When Jonathan had finished, he turned off the lamp and walked over to the box he was looking in previously.

"Can I ask you something?" David asked softly. Jonathan turned around with kind eyes.

"Of course," he responded, returning to his work with the boxes.

"What's the stone say? What's written on it?"

"I believe it is a prophecy from the Prophet Isaiah," Jonathan stated confidently. David walked over next to him and helped him open the box.

"But what's it say in English?" David asked softly.

"Let's see," Jonathan said, returning to the stone and turning back on the lamp. He then translated and read the engraving on the stone in English for David. Jonathan was correct when he said the engraving was from Isaiah, in fact it was the entire chapter, every line, of Isaiah 53. When Jonathan was finished, he turned off the lamp and returned to looking within his box. David, however, remained by the stone and stared at it for a moment.

"Hey! That's talking about Jesus! Wow! Isaiah described Jesus! That's so awesome!" David exclaimed in excitement. Suddenly, his exclamation was interrupted by Jonathan's mother calling the boys up to enjoy some of her tasty brisket dinner.

Once everyone was finished with dessert, which consisted of Jonathan's favorite, his mother's homemade rugelach, Jonathan's father thought it would be a good idea for the boys to go to bed in one of their guest rooms instead of squeezing David into Jonathan's room. When the boys were tired of brainstorming ideas for their cell project, Jonathan's father led them to one of their two large guest bedrooms that contained two single beds. These beds sat across the room from each other on either side with one nightstand and lamp in between them. The boys each dressed in their pajamas, and David entered the room and jumped into his bed first.

Jonathan came in after him and tucked himself in the bed like he did every night in his own bed. Once he was finished, he laid down and tried to sleep, but David interrupted him. "Do you know a lot about the prophets, Jon?"

"Yes, I do," Jonathan answered quickly, trying to sleep. After a pause he moaned with a yawn. "Don't call me Jon."

"Okay, but can I ask you like what?"

With another yawn Jonathan answered, "David, I grew up surrounded by the words of the prophets and of Moses. My family and I have believed in and studied Judaism for centuries. Can I go to sleep now?"

"Wow! That's how you knew how to speak Hebrew and about the Old Testament! I like the Old Testament! I like the part where Moses parts the Red Sea! Hey! Why do they call it the Red Sea? I thought water was blue? Is it red? Is the Red Sea red?"

"Do you always conduct such deep conversations this late at night?" Jonathan moaned, attempting to fall asleep.

"Hey! You know what? I bet we'll get some more ideas 'bout our project tomorrow. You're smart, I think? I mean I don't know for sure." David joked, attempting to keep their conversation going because he wasn't tired yet.

"Simply because I have not come up with the answer to our dilemma does not mean I'm not smart! Besides I haven't seen you coming up with any ideas!" Jonathan shouted sitting up in bed.

"Okay, yeesh! Relax, dude." David laughed. "You know what? I think you're too uptight. You gotta relax, bro!"

"I do relax. I find working on my robots and recreating experiments very enjoyable. Perhaps you are too relaxed, ever think of that?"

"Hey, at least I know how to take a joke." David shrugged. A mischievous smile came across his face as he sneakily grabbed one of his pillows, and when Jonathan laid down to go back to sleep, he flung it at Jonathan's head. The pillow hit Jonathan's head with a lot of force, and Jonathan jumped in surprise. David laughed loudly. With a smile and mischievous eyes, Jonathan grabbed one of his own pillows and threw it at David. David blocked this shot with another pillow. The fight was on. "You call that a throw?" David mocked.

"Says the one hiding on his bed! Way to hit a man while he sleeps!" Jonathan laughed as he began to make a makeshift fort out of his remaining pillows and blankets. To his surprise, David found one of his biggest pillows and charged across the room. He jumped onto Jonathan's bed and began hitting him with the pillow repeatedly and laughing. Jonathan grabbed one of his own pillows and began to fight back, laughing even louder. Soon, his father came to the door and knocked.

"You two better settle down," his father commanded from outside the room.

Jonathan stopped laughing and shouted in response, "Okay, Father!"

David returned to his bed, still chuckling. Once they were both settled, they each wished each other a good night, and they both went to sleep. The next morning was a Friday morning, but thanks to there being a teacher conference that lasted through the whole day, the students at Lancer Middle School did not need to go to school that Friday. David awoke to Jonathan's bed being empty. Jonathan had obviously awoken much earlier than David and had already made his bed. David got up and got dressed. He walked out of the guest room and found his way to Jonathan's bedroom.

He knocked softly and heard a faint voice mumble "Come in." He walked in and saw Jonathan fully dressed, hitting his head against his whiteboard. On his whiteboard, he had drawn a graph with an X, Y, and Z axis to demonstrate their three-dimensional requirement, but other than the graph, there was nothing else to be seen. "I don't understand! This should be exceedingly rudimentary!" Jonathan complained, hitting the whiteboard with his fist.

David could see his friend was troubled, and he greeted him warmly. "Hey, good morning." Jonathan snapped out of his frustration and quickly attempted to remember his manners.

"Oh! Shalom! *Boker tov*! Good morning! I'm sorry for keeping you waiting! Would you like some breakfast?" Jonathan said hurriedly, rushing for the door.

"Sure." David shrugged, following him down the stairs. Minutes later, they were both sitting at Jonathan's dining table, each enjoying a fresh bowl of oatmeal. "It's okay that we don't have it figured out yet. It's not due for like two weeks," David said, leaning back in his chair.

"Actually it's due in exactly twelve days, and that only leaves us one more weekend after this one to complete it," Jonathan moaned, stirring his oatmeal sadly. Jonathan held his head in his hand as he attempted to think of a creative way to make their cell model stand out from the rest.

Simultaneously, David had a different idea. "Hey, maybe we need a break. I got a new video game from Christmas that I haven't played yet. Wanna hang at my place for a while?"

Jonathan lifted his head in surprise. "I don't know?"

David smirked. "It's Astro Comet Racers Five Billion!"

"Astro Comet Racers Five Billion! That just came out a few months ago! I will go ask my parents right now!" Jonathan yelled excitedly, jumping from his seat and running upstairs. His parents said yes as long as David's parents were okay with it. David called Mr. Gardien and asked if it would be all right, and Mr. Gardien thought it would be fine. So David grabbed his bag and thanked Jonathan's parents for their generous, great hospitality, and together Jonathan and David raced over to David's mansion.

Mr. Gardien had left the front gate open for David's return and greeted them at the door once they arrived. Jonathan didn't know David lived in the mansion at the end of his street. He was just as surprised as Abby and Moriah were when they first found out. However, David did not allow him to be in surprise for long. Wanting to play his game, David quickly greeted Mr. Gardien and pulled Jonathan through the greeting area and up to his room. Once inside, David showed him his video game console and video game collection. "You have Target Paint Shooters Unloaded! Volcano Masters! These games are immeasurably cool!"

"I know, right! Let's play!" David said, plugging in the controllers. For the next five hours, various beeps, explosions, boings, dings, splats, and music could be heard outside David's bedroom door. Halfway into their sixth hour mark, Mr. Gardien knocked on the door. "Come in!" David yelled, and Mr. Gardien entered to find two boys completely mesmerized by David's television. Their eyes didn't leave the television screen, even though Mr. Gardien had entered the room, and all the lights were shut off, so they sat in darkness. Snack foods and soda cans that David had brought up were scattered all around.

Mr. Gardien turned on the bedroom light, and the boys flinched as if the light had burned their eyes. "Look at you two! Master David, shouldn't you take a break from that doodad and move around a bit. You've been stuck playing that way for almost an entire day now!"

"What should we do?" David groaned, rubbing his eyes and turning off the video game console. Mr. Gardien paused and thought for a moment.

Then he exclaimed, "How about we find your father's table tennis? He and the Mrs. used to play for hours at that!"

"Table tennis?" David asked.

"You know, where you hit those small balls with the paddles and they bounce over the net in the middle," Jonathan explained. "I'm not very good at it, but I will give it a try."

"Okay, me too!" David shrugged, and together they went downstairs and waited for Mr. Gardien to bring the table. After a while, Mr.

Gardien came rolling the table out and into the front greeting area of the house.

"I'm sure you young men can figure out this little sport while I go upstairs and tidy up the mess you made of your room." Mr. Gardien chuckled.

"Thanks, G-man!" David said, shaking hands with Mr. Gardien. He didn't want to hug him in front of Jonathan. Mr. Gardien in response rubbed his head affectionately, which David always hated because it messed up his hair. After fixing his hair, he picked up one of the paddles and began to play with Jonathan. Jonathan wasn't very good at it, but neither was David since they had just started playing. Nevertheless, the boys had a great time, laughing, dodging, and hitting.

It was in the middle of the afternoon when Jonathan stopped their fourth game short and said, "I have to go. It will be Sabbath soon." He went upstairs and thanked Mr. Gardien for his hospitality, left, and walked toward his house.

David packed up and rolled the table tennis stuff into the parlor and met Mr. Gardien upstairs in his room, still cleaning. "How two boys can manage to make as big a mess as you two did, I'll never know! Soda cans tossed willy-nilly! Popcorn everywhere! My pistachio bag emptied! You don't even like pistachios!"

"No, but Jonathan does. G-man, Jonathan can't work on the Sabbath; that means we can't work on our project tomorrow, and I can't work on it on Sunday because I'll be busy helping and leading worship at church most of the day with Abby and Moriah. What are we gonna do?"

"Work on it after school on Monday. You know you will be busy at church on Sunday because the choir is out of town at that big television choir competition show. The congregation is expecting you, Abigail, and Moriah to sing this Sunday and the one after that for worship. Besides, taking a day to focus on the Lord is a very good practice. Your project can wait." David nodded in agreement and thought about his friend. That Saturday and Sunday David prayed for his friend multiple times, just as he had done every day since they had met.

That Monday after school, David met Jonathan at his house and together they went up to Jonathan's room. "Hey, Jo! I brought my science notes! They're in my backpack!"

"Good, and please don't call me Jo," Jonathan said, beginning to write on his whiteboard some names of organelles. Suddenly, Jonathan turned his head, set his marker down slowly, and turned to face David. "David, when I was in Israel, I had heard of a man named Jesus. You mentioned his name the other day. Who is he?" From their time in the basement, Jonathan had felt a pull on his heart that he couldn't explain. Scriptures he had heard all his life about the coming Messiah were, for a reason Jonathan did not know, stirring in his heart.

So David then went on to share his personal story of coming to know Jesus. Jonathan listened respectfully, and when David had finished by explaining how he was baptized, Jonathan smiled kindly and thanked David for sharing his story with him.

After staring at each other in silence for a moment, Jonathan began to stare at his watch. David then remembered he had his Bible always with him, and even now it was inside of his stylish blue backpack. He pulled out his water-stained little Bible from Pastor Stanson.

"Hey, Jay? Do you want to hear more?" David asked, showing him the Bible.

"I do, and, hmm, Jay? I like that nickname," Jonathan thought out loud as he went to sit next to David on the foot of the bed. David began with the gospel according to Matthew, and from the opening genealogy, Jonathan was interested. Together, they went through all four Gospels, stopping at various points for Jonathan to make connections back to Deuteronomy, the prophets, Psalms, the story of Abraham, or other places in the scriptures. The reality of the text actually made him very alert. He followed David's reading of all four of the Gospels till the end and had a lot to think about. Jesus Christ fulfilled prophecies spoken long ago that Jonathan had studied and memorized ever since his youth. Jesus Christ and the apostles performed miracles that only the Lord could do, and Jonathan recognized that by sacrificing Himself for the sin of the world, Jesus Christ defeated death.

David asked him if he wanted to accept Christ, but Jonathan said he wanted to be left alone. So David went home. Hearing the Gospels was a little overwhelming to Jonathan, and he knew his acceptance of them would have many consequences, but something kept tugging on his heart to remember the words of Jesus.

That week, Jonathan's parents needed to take a five-day trip to Israel to check on one of their excavation sites. They left Monday night and were set to return Sunday morning. Meanwhile, Jonathan's aunt stayed with him in the house and kept the house clean and tidy. She made it a rule that Jonathan couldn't go to any friends' houses or have friends over to his house while she had to keep everything in order. Therefore, David and Jonathan couldn't work on their project for the entire week.

For the rest of the week, Jonathan and David had more work in other classes than ever before and couldn't even begin to think of their cell model project anyway. At school, David kept asking if Jonathan had accepted Jesus, but Jonathan just kept changing the subject. By Sunday, Jonathan had decided, and since his parents had returned and had given him permission, that morning he asked David to come over.

The call to come over so suddenly surprised David, who ran over to Jonathan's house as quick as he could. Together they talked for a while; David didn't have all the answers, but he was able to repeat what his reasons were for having faith in Jesus, and he told Jonathan about the Apostle Paul's story and his faith. David even read Jonathan Paul's letter to the Romans and repeated the gospel to him.

In that moment, Jonathan accepted the Gospels as the Word of God and his life was changed because of the power of the gospel. He realized that because of Jesus's sacrifice, the price for sin was paid and that by believing in Jesus Christ as God and Savior, he could be reconciled with God for all eternity. This meant that the requirements of the Law for righteousness was fulfilled in Jesus Christ, and that by believing in Him and His Word, a believer is then attributed with Jesus's righteousness in the sight of God for all eternity. What David had shared with Jonathan that day and the Monday before that went straight into his heart and gave him a feeling of peace and freedom. He concluded on his own that Jesus Christ is the God of Abraham, Isaac, and Jacob and that Jesus Christ is the Messiah that Israel, including his family, had been waiting for. This was a big deal. Jonathan's parents hadn't come to this conclusion and neither had the rest of Jonathan's family nor the people at Jonathan's synagogue. He didn't know how his family was going to react once they knew he had come to believe in Jesus. However, since Jesus's words were true, his family being disappointed was a risk he had to take. Jonathan and David prayed for Jonathan's salvation, and that day Jonathan was saved. David had bought Jonathan the day before a special Bible with the Old Testament in Hebrew and the New Testament in an English version. He gave it to Jonathan to read and to keep. After that, David went home to have breakfast with Mr. Gardien.

Jonathan thought about what was the best way to tell his parents about Jesus. Suddenly, his mother called to him from downstairs to meet them at their dining room table. Jonathan slowly made his way downstairs and into the dining room. He sat down across from his parents, who were sitting lovingly next to each other. They each were holding each other's arms and smiling. Jonathan coughed and began with "Mom, Dad, there's something I—"

"Wait, Son, there is something very important we have to share with you," his father said with a smile. His mother and father both shared a nervous look; then his father continued. "When we arrived in Israel in the airport, you know the one, it's the same one we used to fly here, we began talking about what had happened before we moved here. You see, before we left a close friend of ours who had grown up in the same city as us told your mother and I how he had come to know Jesus Christ. We've thought about that conversation ever since, and when we arrived in that city a few days ago, we each talked about that conversation. So at that time in Israel, we both made the decision to follow Jesus Christ."

"We were baptized in the Jordan by a local church. It was incredible. So here we are. How do you feel, Jonathan?" his mother asked him. Jonathan's jaw had dropped. He could barely believe what had happened. Half out of surprise and half out of joy, he suddenly began to laugh. He then told his parents how David had shared the gospel with him and how he had become a believer in Jesus Christ. Then all of them were filled with joy and thanked and praised God abundantly. Jonathan read the Bible the rest of the night and after praying before he went to bed; he slept very peacefully that night.

Monday came with a fury. David raced over to Jonathan's house after school, and together they brainstormed their project in his room. Their project was due in only two days. "I'm beginning to theorize we should just give up and buy a foam ball and some modeling clay from the craft store," Jonathan moaned.

"No, we can do this! Okay what are cells? We're made of cells, right?" David thought out loud.

"Yes." Jonathan groaned, placing his hand on his forehead.

"Plants are made of cells, right?"

"A different kind but yes."

David paused and then thought out loud. "So? What are cells made of?"

Jonathan's head shot up, and a huge grin formed on his face. "That's it! Eureka! You figured it out, David!" He shouted, beginning to draw on the whiteboard a bunch of tiny circles. "We can demonstrate how cells are made of biomolecules like proteins. We could build a big half sphere out of an excess amount of smaller spheres, that way it will form a more accurate sphere figure than if we used some other shape. These smaller spheres will be labeled, but where are we going to find a bunch of small, different-colored spheres?"

"Table tennis!" David shouted, jumping to his feet. "I can ask Mr. Gardien for all the table tennis balls we can find, and I'll bring them here!"

"Perfect! Then we can use the markers you brought to write on them and my hot glue to glue them together!" Jonathan smiled, still drawing on his whiteboard their plan. David did just as they had planned, and soon they had a collection of orange, green, pink, and white table tennis balls all glued together forming a large half circle. "Now we need some organelles," Jonathan said to himself, thinking. "A nucleus holds DNA?" Jonathan pondered.

David put on a thinking face as well and asked, "What's DNA look like?"

"It could be partially visually understood as similar to string," Jonathan began to explain but then paused. "I know! I can ask my mom for one of her smaller balls of yarn! She won't mind; it's for a good cause." Jonathan laughed and ran downstairs to ask his mom. In a flash, he returned with a very small ball of light blue yarn that they glued in the center of their half circle. The next two hours were filled with the boys running all over to find different-sized objects for their organelles. David ran to his house and back again a couple times. He donated some broken guitar strings he had saved, since he always hated to throw anything away, and these represented the smooth endoplasmic reticulum. On some of the guitar strings, the boys placed beads to form the rough endoplasmic reticulum. David also donated two chipped guitar picks to be the lysosomes and a few other things he had found. Jonathan donated two large rocks from his childhood rock collection to be the mitochondria. After a while, the boys had all the parts they needed. Their project was created. Then, David borrowed Jonathan's label maker, and while Jonathan directed him, he labeled all the parts on their model. Then, Jonathan created the guide paper on his laptop that also told what each part was. Soon, they were finished completely with their project and just in time with the turn in date only a day away.

On the turn in date, everyone stood outside of Miss Electron's classroom, holding and talking about their cell models. Every single model was creative and interesting, but David and Jonathan's got the most attention. Late again, Miss Electron slowly strolled over to her classroom door and let her students in. "Place all your models on your desk, and I will walk by and judge them based on their creativity." She moaned, sipping her coffee. The students all found their seats in a flash and gently placed their models on their desks. Miss Electron grabbed a clipboard and walked around to each desk to judge the student's work. Everyone held their breath, like gymnasts after performing their routine for the judges. Miss Electron walked slowly to each table and took several moments, touching, examining, and taking notes on each model. David and Jonathan's model was last to be judged. Miss Electron snarled at it as she ran her fingers over the little plastic balls. She quickly wrote down some notes and went up to the front.

All the students sat up straight with anxiety. Some had butterflies in their stomach as they hoped with all their might that they would receive those valuable extra credit points. They all smiled at Miss Electron, hoping to persuade her to pick their model. Taking another sip of her coffee for suspense, she sighed and muttered, "You all did fine work, but in my opinion the most creative model was completed by Mr. Raywood and Mr. Abramson." David and Jonathan jumped out of their seats and cheered. They high-fived and shouted in celebration. Their cell model had won the extra credit points. "They will both receive ten extra credit points added to their overall grade, but because of the fact that all your projects are interesting enough for me to impress the school board with and perhaps earn my well-deserved and overdue raise, you will all receive five extra credit points for your work." The entire class cheered. This was the only day that school year that any happiness was heard from Miss Electron's classroom, and she despised it.

David and Jonathan decided to celebrate at David's house after school with a video game marathon after they finished their other homework. They triumphantly danced into David's room, carrying sodas, bowls of popcorn, and bags of pistachios from Jonathan's house. "We did it! We won!" They cheered and laughed, remembering how hard they had worked. David was about to turn on his game console when he tripped on his guitar case.

"Are you all right?" Jonathan jumped up and helped David to his feet.

"Yeah, I'm okay. Just my extra guitar case."

"You play guitar? Oh! So that's where those metal strings came from?"

"Yep, and I sing. I sing with Abby and Moriah at youth group every Wednesday, and lately I've been singing with them for worship on Sundays 'cause the choir got on some TV show and won't be back for a month," David commented, plugging in the game controllers.

"I wish I could sing skillfully and read music. I've always wanted to learn how to read music. I've heard playing music can decrease, for some individuals, their levels of stress." Jonathan sighed.

"I could teach you?" David offered, handing him a controller.

"I don't know; that would be a lot of work for you." Jonathan laughed.

David thought for a moment and exclaimed, "I know! How 'bout you teach me something in return? Like a trade?"

"What do you want to learn?"

David thought again, and an excited smile came over his face. "How to use the slingshot!" he grinned.

Jonathan laughed. "It's a deal," he said, shaking hands with David. For the next three weeks David taught Jonathan how to sing and how to read music while Jonathan taught David how to hit cans in Jonathan's backyard with the slingshot. They both had lots of fun and lots of frustration. By the end of the three weeks, David was an average shot with the slingshot, and Jonathan was able to sing a whole song moderately well.

After one of their last singing lessons in Jonathan's basement, David had another idea. "Ya know, Jay? I think you should meet Pastor Stanson and Pastor Andy."

"You've told me so much about them, I suppose I should." Jonathan laughed, returning David's songbook to him and taking a sip of root beer.

"How about this Sunday you sing with us on stage?"

Jonathan spat out his root beer and quickly grabbed some tissues to clean it up. "What! Are you crazy?" he coughed, cleaning up the root beer. "I did this for fun! Not for a recital!"

"Moriah told me when she learned to sing her teacher made her do one of those. Come on! It will be fun, and everyone will get to meet you at once! You sing awesome, bro!" David pleaded. Jonathan sighed; he had known David long enough to know the look in his eye when he really wanted something. This was the look he had now, and Jonathan knew he wasn't going to give it up easily.

"One song. Then I never have to sing on stage again?" Jonathan asked in a serious tone.

"Only if you want to." David shrugged. Jonathan laughed at the idea of him ever willingly singing in front of others again.

Reluctantly, he shook David's hand and muttered, "Okay, it's a deal." David cheered and quickly flipped in his songbook, looking for the perfect song for Jonathan to sing.

That Sunday, as the teens came up onto the stage from the back room, Jonathan nervously approached the mic as if it were a snake ready to bite. He was so scared he couldn't even get himself to walk the last three steps to the microphone stand. Gently, David pushed him forward the rest of the way; in return Jonathan turned around and gave him a scowl. David walked up beside him with his guitar and whispered, "Go, you got this." Jonathan looked around him and saw Moriah was in her place at the drums and Abby was in her place at the keyboard. Quickly he removed his glasses, wiped his brow, and placed his glasses back on. With his voice trembling, Jonathan spoke into the microphone.

"Hello," he stuttered, and the microphone made a weird noise that caused the congregation to cover their ears. "Sorry, my name is Jonathan. I'm new to this, and I hope you all like this song. It spoke to my heart and to the heart of my best bud," Jonathan said, looking toward David. David nodded, and just as they had rehearsed, Abby played them in. The song Jonathan had chosen was a modern Christian song about wanting to follow God so closely it was like being God's echo. Trembling, Jonathan began to sing. David began to play his guitar, and Moriah began to play her drums. As he sang, Jonathan's face turned as white as snow, and his hands shook while attempting to hold the microphone stand. For the first couple lines, his voice quivered, so David stepped closer beside him during the sixth line and sang that line with him. Hearing David beside him made Jonathan feel less nervous, and he smiled. He sang the next few lines more confidently, and he began to focus better on the Lord, the one they were worshipping. David began to sing background vocals and started to really get into playing his guitar. Toward the end of the song, there was a small pause where only Abby and Moriah were supposed to play the chorus. During this time David hit Jonathan in the head with a small pebble he had found outside, reminding Jonathan of his slingshot training. Jonathan gave him a glare and laughed. In return, he reached and rubbed David's head, knowing how much that irritated David. When the song was over, the congregation, with Jonathan's parents in attendance, gave them a standing ovation.

The teens all stepped down, but before they were completely off the stage, suddenly Pastor Stanson raced up to the microphone and said, "Thank you, young ones, for that wonderful worship service. As it turns out, our technical supervisor, Brian, in the back, who works the light and sound equipment, just left due to another job opening at the local coffee shop. So I'm afraid we will have to do without my sermon notes on the screen until we can find a replacement."

"I can do it!" Jonathan shouted, raising his hand.

"Are you sure, young man? You can't sing worship and work the soundboard at the same time?"

"Great! I didn't want to sing anymore anyway!" Jonathan cheered, running to the back. Jonathan always had a knack for technology, and he learned the equipment in no time. From then on, that was what Jonathan spent his time doing every Sunday. The church paid him a good amount, and even though he wasn't on stage, Jonathan still sang quietly along to the words while in the back of the sanctuary. After service that Sunday, as Abby, Moriah, David, Jonathan, and the pastor stood outside, the pastor thanked Jonathan immensely.

"So you have just recently come to know Jesus Christ as the Lord of your life? Is that correct from what I've heard from our little sling-shot expert over here," Pastor Stanson commented, rubbing David's head mockingly.

"Will everyone stop messing with my hair!" David yelled, fixing his hair for the third time that morning. Jonathan laughed and nodded his head yes.

"Would you like to be baptized?" the pastor asked. Jonathan paused and thought for a moment. He remembered the speech the Apostle Peter had given in Acts chapter two. He shook his head yes.

Next Sunday, Jonathan came walking down the aisle, dressed in the same type of white robe David and Abigail had worn. The sun was shining, the birds were singing, and the water was ready. Jonathan's parents sat in the front row. David, Abigail, Moriah, and Mr. Gardien also sat in the front row, all dressed in their best clothes, and all excited for their friend. Jonathan entered the water with the pastor.

"Jonathan Abramson, do you believe and trust in Jesus Christ as your Messiah, King, Lord, and Savior?"

"I do."

"Then upon profession of your faith, I now baptize you in the name of the Father, the Son, and the Holy Spirit." The water covered Jonathan completely, and when the waters receded, he knew what he had done was right. The congregation cheered, and after Jonathan had changed back into his regular clothes and talked to his parents, David and Mr. Gardien, along with Abby and Moriah, took Jonathan out to eat to celebrate. On the way, David asked Mr. Gardien to pull over his old jalopy. David, Abigail, Moriah, and Jonathan all exited the vehicle and walked up their peaceful hill to stand in awe at the foot of the cross.

That is how the teens' journeys together began. From then on David, Abigail, Jonathan, and Moriah lived faithful lives to the Lord. Many adventures, which were filled with excitement, comedy, romance, and intrigue, unfolded after their beginnings. Though their stories are fictional, what is the Truth is the Bible, the Word of the Lord.

Until Jesus Christ, the name above all names, comes for His Second Coming, it is my hope that this story blesses your life however He sees fit. He is King over everything, and that is why the darkness shall never overcome the light.

ABOUT THE AUTHOR

E mily Prisk is a Christian author with a Liberal Studies major and a Biblical Studies minor.

Her heart's desire is to help bring others closer to Jesus and to spread the light of God's Word with the world. Her strong Christian values and love of writing bring her work to life in newfound ways.

She began writing this novel at nineteen and hopes that the Lord will use her work to bless the hearts of many around the world.